BEWITCH
LONDON VAMPIRES BOOK 5

◦∞◦

FELICITY HEATON

Copyright © 2012 Felicity Heaton

All rights reserved. No part of this publication may be reproduced, stored in a retrieval system, or transmitted, in any form or by any means mechanical, electronic, photocopying, recording or otherwise without the prior written consent of the publisher, nor be otherwise circulated in any form of binding or cover other than that in which it is published and without a similar condition being imposed on the subsequent purchaser.

The right of Felicity Heaton to be identified as the Author of the Work has been asserted by her in accordance with the Copyright, Designs and Patents Act 1988.

First printed August 2019

Second Edition

Layout and design by Felicity Heaton

All characters in this publication are purely fictitious and any resemblance to real persons, living or dead, is purely coincidental.

THE LONDON VAMPIRES SERIES

Book 1: Covet

Book 2: Crave

Book 3: Seduce

Book 4: Enslave

Book 5: Bewitch

Book 6: Unleash

**Discover more available paranormal romance books at:
http://www.felicityheaton.com**

Or sign up to my mailing list to receive a FREE vampire romance ebook, learn about new titles, be eligible for special subscriber-only giveaways, and read exclusive content including short stories:
http://ml.felicityheaton.com/mailinglist

CHAPTER 1

This was the last place on earth that Payne wanted to be.

The heavy iron gate squeaked as it closed behind him. Slippery, damp stone steps led downwards into the gloom. Payne allowed his eyes to change to reveal his vampire nature, his irises burning red and his pupils turning elliptical, and the tunnel brightened enough for him to make out the arching roof cut into the rock.

Noises came from ahead.

He followed the steps in a sweeping curve, his footfalls echoing around him. His breaths formed as white fog in the moist air before dissipating. A golden glow crept into view further down the tunnel and a gust of drier air washed over him, carrying a myriad of scents. Herbs. Spices. Dead things. Blood. Other disgusting fetid smells joined them as he continued to descend and he wished that vampires didn't feel the need to breathe.

The steps ended and he followed the uneven earth floor. The tunnel grew larger until it opened onto a high plateau at the start of a cavern. His eyes switched back to their normal grey and the world dulled to a more manageable level of brightness.

Enormous rust-coloured stalactites hung from the ceiling arching above him, as though the cave had grown fangs, rows of them, all sharp and wicked in the golden glow rising up from below. Their menacing shadows stretched long across the roof, adding to the sense of danger that he liked. He could live in a place like this. A vampire liked mystery. It was perfect for his kind.

Or it would be if it weren't for the thousands of fae that bustled in the small underground town spread out below him.

Stone buildings covered the huge base of the cavern, a hotchpotch collection of square flat-roofed structures of different heights. Some were two storeys but most of them were a single level, with large windows and tattered canopies reaching out from them into the narrow streets, each a different jewel-tone colour. Some of the ones directly below him bore crests or fae words he didn't understand. Alleys wound between the stores and homes in stilted lines that reminded Payne of veins. His stomach growled a reminder that he hadn't eaten in days, not since he had started out from Vampirerotique on this ridiculous mission.

Scents rose from copper stills, thatched baskets, vials and terracotta or stone jars that stood on display outside the stores on his left, and a wooden arch at the start of one of the streets declared it was the witches' district. Fae and other creatures crammed the streets, passing from store to store. There had to be close to five thousand fae and other creatures in the area.

Payne studied them, an increasing sense of dread churning in his stomach.

Witches didn't like vampires. His kind had almost driven them to extinction many centuries ago and they hadn't forgiven them for it.

Still, he had to go down there. He had made a promise and he intended to keep it. He smiled to himself as he thought about the succubus who needed his help. She had chosen to call herself Chica. Andreu, her lover and one of the vampires who worked at the erotic London theatre with Payne, had explained that it was a pet name that he had called her a few times. Payne couldn't blame her for keeping her real name secret. He knew firsthand the danger of giving your true name to someone.

Chica needed a way to break the spell that bound her to the theatre, Vampirerotique, stopping her from ever leaving its walls. They had tried everything over the past few weeks and none of it had worked.

Antoine, the vampire in charge of the theatre, was at the end of his tether and the dark aristocrat didn't need this extra burden on his shoulders. He had enough to deal with.

Callum had brought a very heavily pregnant Kristina to the theatre, moving the werewolf into his apartment there, and then Snow had taken a turn for the worse three weeks ago, shortly after Javier and Lilah had married at Vampirerotique.

Payne smirked.

It hadn't quite been the wedding that Javier had envisioned for his lovely bride, but Lilah had wanted everyone there, including Snow and Antoine, and Andreu. Andreu, Javier's younger brother, hadn't wanted to leave Chica alone at the theatre with Snow and Antoine in order to travel to Spain, so Javier had brought his whole family to the theatre to wed his bride on the stage. It had been tasteful enough. They had since left to hold the traditional celebrations in northern Spain at the family's mansion there.

Chica had been miserable then because Andreu had again refused to leave her and she felt it was her fault that he was missing his brother's wedding celebrations. Andreu had done his best to reassure her and Payne had reiterated his promise to help her and free her of the binding spell. He'd had more luck in his latest search for a way of undoing it, managing to find three potential leads, all of them in the fae world.

One of those leads had landed him in trouble.

One had refused to speak to a half-breed. That had pissed Payne off no end. He had told the shapeshifter that he was a vampire but the male had focused on the incubus side of his genes. Payne had felt like killing him but had let it go. Dead or alive, the man wouldn't have been any help.

The final lead had brought him here, to a whole fae town hidden beneath the grounds of an elegant palatial mansion in the English countryside. Fae lived in the mansion too, the elite of the light side of that world. Everyone down here were merchants, plying their wares to make ends meet, or workers and travellers. Payne had thought witches had higher standards but there were probably hundreds if not thousands of them here, trading with other creatures, selling spells, ointments and god only knew what else.

A group of three young females reached the top of the stone steps to his left and passed him, dressed in the traditional garb of witches, long black featureless dresses that swamped their bodies and concealed their curves. They tittered amongst themselves, their eyes on him, blushes heating their cheeks. His incubus side rose to the fore and he shot them a smile, earning giggles and a few sultry smiles in return. The incubus in him loved every second, lapping up their desire, draining it from the air around him.

Payne tamped it down and his vampire side took control again. The witches' looks turned dark and he knew they had seen the red in his eyes. Strange how they would toy with an incubus, one who wanted them purely for sexual gratification, but they would scowl at a vampire. His incubus nature was more likely to kill them.

He took the steps on the left down to the cavern floor, his eyes on the town, studying it. There were larger buildings near the edges of the town. Banners hung on their walls. He recognised a few. Not just covens. There was a shapeshifter pride. A wolf pack. Ogres too. There was even a succubus clan. He didn't need to recognise the banner on that particular building to know what type of creature lived within its dark red walls. There was a steady stream of men coming and going, and some succubi were hanging out of the open windows, calling to them and teasing them with flashes of flesh. The fae equivalent of a bordello.

He shook his head and focused back on the witches' district. He was shit out of luck if the street signs were in fae. The fae language was extensive and his knowledge of it was limited. He knew the basics but names were often written in a special way. He had never learned those characters.

He looked down at the line of markings that tracked up the underside of his forearms and disappeared beneath the charcoal grey rolled up sleeves of his shirt. The swirls, dashes and spikes shifted in hues of dark blue and burnished gold. Not a sign of his incubus side. His markings shone bright gold and cerulean when that was in control. No, this was apprehension.

Understandable considering he was about to enter a world that prided itself on bloodlines and purity.

An abomination like him was liable to end up deep in shit. He wasn't sure which role to play. The vampire or the incubus? They were more likely to accept his demonic lineage and most of the creatures in the area he needed to head into were unlikely to be able to sense the vampire in him.

Incubus it was.

He hated that.

He reached the bottom of the stone steps and the crowd immediately swallowed him. Women dressed in very little tossed provocative looks his way and his incubus side purred from their attention. He wanted to tamp it down but his vampire side had a tendency to show when he forced it to the fore to obliterate his incubus hungers. He couldn't risk them seeing he had a dual personality.

Payne preened his long fingers through the dirty blond spikes of his hair and the women hissed at him and disappeared in a flash, teleporting out of his presence.

Fairly standard behaviour for a succubus when it saw an incubus.

He grinned to himself, remembering how Chica had reacted to him in such a way when she had first come to the theatre. Succubi were weaker than incubi, and it had led to the incubi taking advantage of them more than once, and trying to kill them too. It seemed both sides of his genes had trampled on the feelings of other species without remorse.

He found his first street sign at a junction between four shops all selling herbs that stung his nose. Each plump female owner stood outside, trying to outshout the others. Payne covered his sensitive ears and glared at the wooden post in the middle of the busy crossroads and the boards pointing in different directions.

Just as he had expected. He was shit out of luck.

He didn't recognise any of the symbols on the wooden boards. He jammed his hands in his jeans pockets and not just because he was frustrated. He had been bumped more than once and he was damned if he was going to have his wallet nicked. That would be the turd icing on a crap cake.

A woman with milk white skin and hair the colour of snow approached him, the crowd parting to allow her through. Her starlight coloured robes flowed ethereally around her, revealing more than they were concealing. She looked like a ghost. Payne stood his ground, his vampire senses sparking high alert, and steadied himself. Every instinct said to roar and scare her away.

Phantom.

He had never seen one before but he had heard that a phantom's touch could make a man incorporeal. A phantom too. It was the only way for one such as her to mate. She needed to make her male as intangible as she was. When he had first heard that, it had sounded as though it might be fun. Then he had learned that once a phantom, always a phantom. The male never got his corporeal status back and was destined to roam the world as a hollow husk when the phantom cast him aside. No way was he signing up for that.

Her palest silver eyes slid to him and she held her hands out.

Payne reacted on instinct, his eyes darkening to crimson and his pupils turning elliptical. He bore his lengthening fangs at her and growled. She halted and even moved back, but she didn't leave. She stared at him and her white lips moved. No sound left them but he heard her words in his head.

Unfortunately, he didn't understand most of them. He caught fae words for 'fated', 'bond', 'blood' and 'death'.

Before he could ask her in English what she had said to him and what it meant, she swirled into smoke and disappeared. He looked around at the people now staring at him, his skin crawling from their attention and the way they were looking at him as though the phantom had just announced his death sentence. He let his fangs recede and his eyes change back to dark grey, and then singled out one of the witches who had stopped to stare.

"What did she say?"

The woman frowned at him, turned her back and went about her business. Just great. It seemed their looks of horror were because he had flashed his vampire nature. No one else had heard what the phantom had told him and he was damned if he could remember what she had said to repeat it to them.

He didn't need this shit on top of everything else.

Payne stared at the street sign and decided to go left. He was feeling in a sinister mood after all.

He reached another crossroads and was in the process of deciding which route to take next when a huge cloud of sparkling grey dust exploded into the air off to his right. People ran from that direction, pushing past him. He braced himself and frowned over their heads. There was a shape in the dust, small and curvy, and she wasn't alone. Four larger shapes surrounded her.

That didn't seem like a fair fight to Payne.

He ran towards the fray and broke through the dust. Storeowners screamed at the fighters, some of them ferrying their wares inside where it was safe and others standing in front of them, physically protecting them.

The female he had seen through the cloud of dust stood her ground before him, feet spread shoulder width apart beneath the hem of her drab black dress, the long chestnut waves of her hair tangled in the pieces of straw sticking out of it. Grey dust sparkled across her backside. She must have hit whatever had exploded and sent the dust into the air.

Four large males stood opposite her, each of them hunkered low, assessing her.

They were witches too, judging by the coven emblem stitched onto the breast of their loose white shirts and the fact they were all wearing matching dark brown trousers, like a uniform. Payne raised an eyebrow at the elaborate lacing down the front of their shirts, and on their trousers.

Where had their coven bought their outfits? Or when for that matter?

They looked like something straight out of the eighteenth century. Although, the female of their species didn't exactly dress in modern attire either. His gaze slid back to her, slowly taking in her dull black dress, trying to pierce the material to see what curves it concealed.

One of the men shuffled, bracing his feet shoulder-width apart on the cobblestones, preparing to attack.

What did they want with the female?

Her heartbeat was frantic. Frightened.

One of the males lunged at her and she turned on the spot, threw herself forwards and rolled towards Payne. She found her feet just a few metres in front of him and her eyes widened as they met his. Smudges of black ash dotted her pale face but Payne didn't notice them.

She was beautiful.

Entrancing.

Her silvery eyes sparkled like stars.

The male grabbed her from behind and leaned back, lifting her feet off the floor. She unleashed a low growl of frustration and landed a series of devastating blows on him. Her foot slammed into the man's left knee, hobbling him, and then she jammed her elbow into his face, right into his eye. Payne winced when the man howled and dropped the petite firecracker and she turned and landed a hard kick to his balls. The man hit the deck, clutching himself and groaning.

The sight of her so easily dispatching their comrade didn't stop the other three. They attacked as one with magic, hurling colourful sparkling orbs that caught her right in the chest and sent her flying. She tumbled through the air, the skirt of her dress hiking up to reveal sinfully red knickers. Payne had intended to catch her but the sight of them froze him right to his boots. His incubus purred. The vampire in him purred too.

The female landed hard in the baskets outside one of the stores to his left, scattering their contents. Snakes slithered over the cobbles and frogs hopped, making a break for freedom. Payne lifted his left boot to allow a black and red snake to pass. The elderly witch who owned the store added insult to injury and beat the poor female with a broom. The beauty got to her feet by rolling unceremoniously into the cobbled street, her dress still tangled around her middle, flashing her knickers and a lot of smooth creamy leg.

He wasn't the only one the sight of her had enchanted. The three males were all dumbstruck too, staring at her exposed skin.

She got to her feet, grabbed a length of thin silver rope that had fallen from one of the baskets, and brandished it like a whip.

She lashed out at the males, cracking the end of the rope across their chests and legs. The males reacted then, each making vain attempts to close the distance between them. Even teleportation spells didn't help them. She struck them before they could fully disappear, stopping them.

Payne stared. The sight of her with the makeshift whip, dominating the more powerful males with it, was arousing to say the least. He knew his eyes were glowing blue and gold, and he knew he should get his hungers under control before they took him over and made him do something he might regret, but by god almighty he wanted the little witch.

One of the males managed to reach her and caught the hand that held the rope. The others looked ready to pile in. It was going to get out of hand.

Payne felt a strange urge to protect her.

He leaped into the fray, barrelling into the man who had captured her and taking him down. He slammed a right hook into his cheek, felt bone give and then crack under the force of the blow. The man bellowed in pain and he struck him again, breaking his jaw. The enticing scent of blood filled the air and Payne growled. His hunger rose.

The female was back in action, hurling vicious magical attacks at the other two males, shrieking at them in the fae tongue. When he had made a vague effort to learn the language, Payne had followed the tradition of all language students and started with the swear words. She cursed better than any of those clichés. Sailors, soldiers and troopers had nothing on this woman.

One of the males grabbed Payne from behind, hauling him off the other witch. He snarled, quickly turned and caught the man with a hard right uppercut and then a left hook as the man dropped him. He kept dealing blows, driving the man away from the female.

A bolt of something blue shot past Payne and sent the male he had been fighting flying through the air. The man smacked into the side of one of the buildings, rolled awkwardly down the emerald green canopy and landed hard on the cobbled street.

The other man fled, helping one of the injured. The fourth man hobbled past Payne and he growled at him, allowing his eyes to blaze red and fangs to lengthen enough that the man got the hint.

The four males looked back past him, to the female. They said something in fae. Payne caught a few words as his fangs receded and his eyes changed back to grey, enough to know they intended to tell on her to their coven. Had she done something wrong?

Payne turned to face her.

She stood in the middle of the narrow street, her silver eyes dark with determination, her breathing as rapid as her heartbeat. Payne took a step towards her and she lashed out at him with the rope. He easily caught the end of it before it could strike him.

Payne stared at her. She struggled with the rope, trying to pull it free of his grip, her pretty face twisting in anger and her eyes bright with it too. Hay stuck out of her long chestnut hair in places, the tousled waves resembling more of a bush than the beautiful glossy locks they had been before her tumble in the baskets and beating with a broom. She looked like a wild animal, feral and vicious.

Payne wanted to tame her.

He held her attention. The sparks of silver in her striking eyes brightened. He took a step towards her, gathering the rope at the same time, keeping it taut between them. She raised her other hand and a golden orb glowed close to her palm. She didn't want to let him near her. He got the message and ignored it too. He kept moving towards her, steady steps, his eyes constantly locked on hers. He could see she didn't want to lower that magic or let him close to her, even as he worked to change it. He hated to use his natural talents on anyone but she was going to get herself killed if he didn't get her off the street soon. Those males would come back with more like them.

She blinked slowly. Payne lost focus as her long dark lashes shuttered her incredible eyes, stealing them from view. The distraction cost him. She smiled and yanked the rope. It slipped from his grasp and she lashed out with it, catching him hard across the cheek. He didn't flinch, didn't take his eyes off her. The smell of his blood mixed with the scents in the air.

Payne kept slowly advancing, his eyes on hers, keeping them riveted on him. She wanted to give up her fight. She wanted him. He sent that feeling to her, filling her mind with thoughts of them together, trying to convince her to lower her guard.

She drew her arm back to strike again.

Payne teleported just as she let loose with the rope and appeared right in front of her. He caught her wrists, his eyes still on hers. She stared up at him, her sensual rosy lips parted in shock and her eyes dark with desire that swirled into him through the point where they touched, feeding his hunger. Her breathing quickened to short soft pants. He had never heard anything so erotic and alluring. He wanted to hear her panting like that into his ear as he thrust into her welcoming wet heat.

"I won't hurt you," he whispered and her pupils dilated. "Give in to me."

He felt her relax. Her fingers opened and the rope fell from them.

Her dark eyebrows drew together and her pupils narrowed. She yanked her right hand free of his grip and slammed her fist into his cheek, splitting open the gash there from the whip. Payne grabbed her wrist again and held them both in a bruising grip. It seemed she was a little immune to his charm.

"I won't hurt you," he repeated and her struggling slowed until she was wriggling against him in a way that fired him up.

He shoved her away and scowled at her. She blinked into his eyes and then dropped her gaze to his hands where they clutched her wrists. It rose to his cheek and she stilled.

"You're bleeding." She spoke in English, her voice soft and light, full of warmth that curled through him, easing his tension.

Was his charm offensive getting through to her now? He focused on her and his incubus side didn't purr. Evidently not.

She pulled her hand free of his and gently pressed the pads of her fingers to the skin below the cut on his cheek. Payne hissed in a sharp breath, heat flooding him, all stemming from the point where she touched him. He stared down into her silver-grey eyes, hungry thoughts spinning through his mind, his body reacting swiftly.

She broke free of him, a soft gasp escaping her sinful mouth and her cheeks darkening. Had she sensed his thoughts? She smoothed her plain black dress, looking for all the world as if she was doing her best to smooth her feelings with it. Her heartbeat was all over the place and he could sense her desire.

"Come with me."

She didn't wait for a response. She turned her back, picked up the rope, and walked away, heading towards the crossroad he had come from. Payne raked his gaze over her, the oversized black dress hiding none of her from his imagination now. He had seen her shapely legs and crimson knickers, and he still burned from that brief glimpse. She plucked a piece of straw from her hair and glanced over her shoulder at him, her beautiful eyes immediately capturing his attention. He was supposed to have cast a spell on her to get her under his control.

He felt as though she had cast one on him.

Payne followed her, unable to resist his need to know her taste and her touch. He could never allow it to happen though.

He couldn't influence her.

She was immune.

Immunity to an incubus's charms was a sign that she was their fated mate.

The last woman who had been semi-immune to his charms had broken his heart.

The phantom's words came back to him.

Fated. Bond. Blood. Death.

Sounded like a recipe for disaster to him, and this little witch was just the first ingredient.

CHAPTER 2

Payne used the walk to get his hunger back in check. He would go with the witch to wherever she was leading him, gain her trust and then get her to tell him the location of the place he sought. She could speak fae and others knew her here, so she clearly knew the area well. She would be able to lead him to his destination. Problem solved.

He tried to keep his eyes off her backside.

It was impossible.

The image of saucy red knickers had been burned on his mind.

He would never look at witches the same again. Who knew what they hid beneath that plain boring black dress? He had never imagined it would be naughty knickers.

She turned down another street to her left, leading him through the rabbit warren of buildings. There were fewer stores in this neighbourhood. Most of the single storey buildings looked like residences, most of them painted in bright colours. Stalagmites rose from the flat roofs of many of them, reaching upwards towards their deadly counterparts on high.

Payne stopped a few steps into the new narrow street and backtracked. He raised a single dark eyebrow at the wooden sign affixed to the painted black wall of the building nearest the crossroads. Well, what did'ya know. He took a piece of paper from his pocket and matched the symbols to those of the street name. Bingo. We have a winner.

The witch had stopped and was staring at him, curiosity burning in her silvery eyes.

He didn't need her after all.

He stalked past her, checking each door for the right symbol. Somewhere down here was the witch he had come to find. His eyes darted from the crumpled piece of paper in his hand to the painted purple wooden door of the pink stone building on his left. Match.

He rapped his knuckles against the door.

The female witch stopped beside him. He glanced at her. She was frowning now and it didn't suit her. He didn't like how she looked as though she was trying to see right through him to wheedle out his secrets.

He opened his mouth to explain himself.

She slid a brass key into the lock, twisted it and pushed the door open. She breezed into the dark building and lights came on, glowing warmly and illuminating the clutter in the small room.

She lived here?

She was the witch?

She tossed the key and silver rope onto a messy wooden desk on the right of the room. A fire burst into life in the grate to his left, near two tattered armchairs. A dark threadbare rug spread across the stone floor between them, covered in haphazard piles of books.

Payne closed the door behind him. The witch bustled through into an adjoining room and returned with a hairbrush that she put to good use, viciously dragging it through her tangled hair.

She didn't flinch when it caught on knots and pieces of hay. She grumbled in the fae language, dark things that had Payne remaining close to the exit. She was livid about something. He could feel her anger in her blood and hear it in her heartbeat, and sense it in other easier ways too. The fire on the grate roared like an inferno and the flames on the candles were six inches tall and blazing white, evidently a response to her rage.

She paced, heeled black leather ankle boots loud on the stone floor.

Whoever those males had been, she was pissed as hell at them.

Payne leaned his back against the wall and breathed slowly. She wasn't a threat to him. He focused on the calm ebbing and flowing through him, trying to instil that same feeling in her, and raised his hand to his face. He was still bleeding. He licked the blood from his fingers and then licked them again and dabbed his saliva across the cut.

She stopped pacing then and tossed the brush onto one of the dark red armchairs. It bounced off the cushion and landed on the fire. She cursed, shrugged, and approached him. She looked different with all the tangles and twigs gone from her chestnut hair, but she still had a wildness about her, a wickedness that Payne found alluring.

The witch stopped in front of him. He looked down at her. She was petite, a good nine inches shorter than he was.

"Elissa." She offered her hand. He didn't take it. It had been hard enough dealing with skin contact in the street. If he touched her now, when they were alone, in private, he probably wouldn't be able to stop his hunger from rising again. If that happened, he would have her on that bed he could see in the adjoining room and naked in under five seconds. She frowned into his eyes. "Thank you for helping me..."

Clever ploy. She wanted his name.

"Payne."

It seemed she wasn't satisfied with his aloof air and refusal to place her at risk by touching her. She tiptoed and touched the cut on his cheek.

Payne felt that same intense gut-tugging jolt as he had the first time they had made skin contact.

Warmth crept outwards from where she touched, turning him hazy, drugging him with how good it felt. His very nature said to go with the flow because the flow felt divine. The little witch could give him what he needed. Not just the method of freeing Chica from her bond. She could give him bliss.

He could feed on both her energy and her blood.

His incubus side and his vampire one purred at the prospect.

His cut stung and he could almost feel his flesh knitting back together. Magic.

"Witch," he growled, a low warning that he didn't like her meddling with his body.

She didn't heed it but she did eventually withdraw her hand. She smiled up at him. "Sort of."

"Sort of?" He frowned at her. How could you be sort of a witch?

"I don't have much power yet. I'm still learning." Her sweet voice was a melody in his ear, curling around him, petting him and feeding his desire.

She stepped back, distancing herself. His eyes must have changed again, swirling blue and gold. Payne lifted his hand and grazed the backs of his fingers across her soft cheek, his breath shuddering in his chest over how exquisite she felt. He wanted her.

She knocked his hand away. "Don't turn on the charm. I don't like it."

That brought Payne back to earth with a bump. "You can tell when I'm using my ability?"

She nodded and moved back another step. "I don't like it. It feels as though I'm seeing myself do things, feel things, that aren't really anything to do with me."

Strange. Was it a witch thing? He hadn't heard that immune females could sense an incubus attempting to use his ability on her. It had to be a witch thing.

"Normally people can't tell it isn't their natural feelings." His gaze tracked her across the room.

"I'm not normal now, am I?" She stared into the fire and sighed at her melting hairbrush. At least the flames had died down. Her heartbeat was level again too and he couldn't feel any anger in her.

She looked back over her shoulder at him, her eyes locking with his, their dazzling silver depths enchanting him once more. Her lips parted and her pupils dilated. Desire. He could get drunk on the way she felt whenever she looked at him. How would she feel if he took things further?

"I don't like it," she said in a breathless voice. "I don't know why you feel the need to use it... so stop it."

Payne smiled. "I'm not right now."

Her eyes widened and she blinked. "You aren't?"

He shook his head. "Whatever you're feeling, it's one hundred percent yours, and I'm flattered."

She turned her nose up at him. "Get over yourself."

His smile widened into a grin when her heart skipped a beat and her cheeks turned rosy.

She disappeared into the bedroom again and slammed the door behind her. Payne listened to her stomping around the room and muttering about him. He cast a glance around the messy room, studying the piles of books, the vials and beakers, and bottles of coloured liquids and jars of herbs and other more questionable things. A witch's home was disappointingly close to what he had imagined.

Elissa emerged from the bedroom.

The witch however, was nothing like he had pictured.

She had changed into a pair of tight black jeans and a sexy purple halter-top that gathered beneath her breasts, and by god, she wasn't wearing a bra. He could see the soft buds of her nipples pressing against the material. The chestnut waves of her long hair curled around her milky shoulders and a black choker with a silver star in the centre ringed her throat. Payne swallowed, desire surging through him, hot and heavy, burning up his blood.

Was she trying to kill him?

"I thought witches wore those dull black dresses?" he said and was that his voice that had sounded squeaky and tight?

He cleared his throat.

She smiled wickedly, her lips a glossy pink now, enticing him more than ever. "I was on duty... now I'm off duty."

"I need you on duty." And not just because off-duty Elissa was hotter than Hell on a summer's day and had all his blood rushing to his cock.

"Why?" She twirled the ends of her hair and stared at him, her silvery eyes bright with curiosity again.

"I came to this place to speak to you. I need an item for a friend of mine. She's a fae and was accidentally bound to a theatre. I heard you can help us."

"Sounds like a real problem." Elissa thoughtfully tapped her finger against her chin, drawing his gaze to those glossy tempting lips. Would they taste sweet if he kissed her? She shook her head. "But I'm only covering for the witch who normally lives here. Sort of like house sitting."

Payne's insides dropped a few inches. Not good. He was shit out of luck just as he had feared and the witch she was covering for had been his last lead. It was back to the books and the research. He hated the thought of returning to Vampirerotique empty handed. He wouldn't be able to bear the look of disappointment on Chica and Andreu's faces when they discovered he had failed them again, and god only knew how long it would be before he turned up more leads and more potential fixes for their problem.

He heaved a sigh and scrubbed his hand through his blond hair. "Thanks for your time."

He grabbed the door handle and pushed down, letting the door swing open. It was probably for the best anyway. He wasn't sure how much longer he could last around Elissa without pouncing on her and getting that taste he hungered for.

"You're in luck." Those words stopped him dead and he turned back to her.

"I am?"

She nodded, looking very bright and cheerful. It set him on edge. He didn't like that she was smiling at him. It made him feel as though she was up to something, was plotting behind those beautiful eyes. He could almost see the wheels in her mind turning.

"I can help you better than Verity could have... but I have a price."

He knew it. She was up to something. "What?"

She nibbled her lower lip and crossed the room to him, moving so close that personal space became an issue and he had to take a step back to avoid her body pressing into his. She looked up into his eyes, hers surrounded by sinful black kohl that highlighted how silver they were and enhanced the devastating power they held over him. He couldn't look away, even when his gut instinct was to run before she answered because he already knew he wasn't going to like her reply.

"I want a taste of you, Incubus."

"No fucking way." The only way he could distance himself was to back out into the street.

Elissa didn't look pleased. Her expression darkened and then lightened again in the space of a heartbeat. She shrugged.

"It was worth a try." Those words gave him the distinct impression that she really needed his help with a different matter and had been trying to sweeten the deal by getting a taste of him. His incubus side kicked off at that, disgustingly pleased by the fact that she wanted him. Desire surged through him, hunger to taste her too and see if she was as sweet as she looked. Payne tamped it down, unwilling to surrender to that urge.

She backed off, moving to the fireplace. He flinched when she poked it with a fire iron and shoved the dark memories it evoked to the back of his mind. His right forearm throbbed and he was holding it before he realised what he was doing.

Payne stepped back into the small building.

Elissa put the fire iron down, much to his relief, and settled herself in the armchair facing him.

"Tell me what you know about curing my friend's problem." He remained near the door, his gaze locked on her, monitoring her for a sign that she was lying about any of this—her feelings and her ability to help him. Her heartbeat remained level.

"There's a ring that can bind a fae to someone."

Payne's breath left him on a sharp exhale. "It exists?"

She nodded. "It's real alright and I've seen it."

He had heard of such a ring, one powerful enough to overrule any other bond, but he had thought it was a myth. None of his research into it had turned up anything to indicate it was real, so he hadn't pursued it as a possible solution for Chica. If he could get his hands on it, Andreu could use it to bind Chica to him, freeing her of her bond to the theatre. Payne was sure she would happily go along with being bonded to her mate.

Elissa toed her heeled short black boots off and brought her feet up onto the seat of her armchair, tucking them close to her bottom. Red knickers. Payne tried not to stare. It was hard to keep his eyes on her face when all they wanted to do was drop a few feet and stare at her backside, imagining the naughty lingerie the jeans concealed.

The incubus side of him purred. Damn, she was wreaking havoc on him.

"I know where the ring is and that's where you come in. The man who has it also has something of value that belongs to me, something dear to my heart. I want it back. You'll be perfect for helping me achieve that."

Payne folded his arms across his chest. His forearms tensed against the rolled up sleeves of his dark grey shirt. "Why?"

"Because the man is also an incubus."

Payne resisted his desire to growl at her. "I don't see how I will be much help with that."

She stared at him, her right eyebrow slowly rising. "You really don't have a freaking clue about yourself, do you? I had thought I was reading you wrong..."

Payne glared at her. He knew all he needed to know about himself. He was an abomination and he hated this world. He wanted to go back to his world.

He did not want to meet another incubus.

There were two other reasons he didn't want to help her. One, he couldn't control her for some reason and it was unsettling him, especially with that phantom's words still ringing in his ears. Being around Elissa was too enticing. Two, she was right and he didn't know much about incubi and he hated to go into any situation blind.

Diversionary tactics were required. He knit his eyebrows together and pinned her with a scowl. "Did you try to fuck that male too?"

Elissa tensed, flew from the armchair and slapped him hard across his left cheek, snapping his head to his right. The scent of fresh blood cut through the herbs and spices in the air. She had reopened the wound.

"No!" She huffed and looked as though she was considering hitting him again. If she tried it, he was going to hit her back. He was all for equal rights. "And if I had, I certainly wouldn't be asking you for help."

Payne rubbed his stinging cheek. "Why not?"

She grabbed his arm, sending another hot bolt of lust through him, and twisted it. She pointed near his wrist.

"Because he's your grandfather."

Payne tugged his arm free of her grip and turned it so he could see the markings on his skin. She prodded several symbols in a row. That was his grandfather's name? Were his fae markings a record of his bloodline?

That made him hate them all the more.

He stared at the swirling glyphs, a low growl rumbling through him, anger that poured into his veins like acid and ate away at the restraints tethering his temper and his pain. His grandfather. His pulse accelerated, heart thumping hard against his breastbone, driving that scalding acid through his body, cranking up his anger to new, dangerous heights. Grandfather. He wanted to scratch those markings off his arm, loathed them with all of his being. He didn't want to know that somewhere out there was the bastard who had sired his mother, who in turn had spawned him. An abomination.

Devil, he wanted that man to pay for his sins. He wanted to erase his grandfather's name from his lineage and then erase him from existence.

Elissa released an exasperated huff. "You really don't know anything about your kind, do you?"

He growled at her. "My kind are vampires."

Her eyes shot wide. "What on mother earth did you just say?"

Payne towered over her and growled down at her again, his lips peeling back to reveal his fangs. "I'm a vampire."

She stared at his mouth, eyes enormous and pulse off the scale. "What you are is all shades of messed up."

He shoved her away from him. She tripped on a stack of books and landed in the pile behind them, her right arm catching on the armchair and her legs splayed. Payne tried not to think about her naked and like that, spread for his pleasure, the chestnut curls at the apex of her thighs glistening with arousal.

Tried and failed.

It had clearly been too long since he'd had sex.

A good century at least. Damn.

He was a ticking time-bomb of lust. He had heard tales of incubi who had gone insane from lack of sexual gratification. Payne looked down at his right hand. It was probably the only thing keeping him sane, but the pleasure he took from masturbation didn't come close to the satisfaction he gained from intercourse.

Intercourse with this witch was officially off the menu though.

"You need to work on that temper." She winced and pulled herself back onto her feet. "You need my help if you want to get that ring. Remember that."

"Just tell me where he is and I'll find him without you." He wasn't in the mood for this. She had crossed the line and he wanted to get the hell away from her. He should've known better. A pretty thing like her would want nothing to do with a monster like him.

"You won't be able to find him without my help."

"Draw me a map." He was not going to change his mind about this, no matter what she did. "I'll get the ring and whatever piece of junk you want me to bring back for you."

She folded her arms across her chest, squashing her breasts into cleavage that made his heart thump against his ribs for a completely different reason. Her lips compressed into a mulish line, her eyebrows drawing tight.

"If you want to get that ring, you will need to learn about your incubus side. I need what that bastard took from me... I can help you with your incubus side." Those words chilled him.

"Why do I need to?" He didn't want to learn about his incubus side. He already knew enough. It was a curse.

She stacked the books back into messy piles. "Incubi don't live in places that are easy to find. They live in places only accessible by incubi. You'll need to teleport me there and you'll need to do something else too."

"What?" Payne didn't like the sound of this. His day had looked good but it was rapidly going downhill and he had a feeling it was about to get much worse.

"You need to pretend I'm your mate."

Payne stared at her, his mouth dry and heart frozen in his chest.

She couldn't know that she was potentially just that to him.

The wicked gleam in her eyes and the sensual tilt of her glossy lips warned that she wanted more than make believe from him. He could see what she desired and he couldn't give it to her. He wouldn't let his darker nature out to play and he certainly wasn't about to masquerade as her lover or enter a den and face his grandfather. He wanted nothing to do with his incubus nature. He wished it didn't exist.

He couldn't do this.

He turned to leave.

Elissa was there before him, her hands braced against the doorframe, blocking his exit. There was a decidedly different look on her face now. She had gone from stubborn, determined and wicked, to scared, desperate and weak. What was it that she wanted him to retrieve for her? Whatever it was, it looked as though it meant the world to her.

"This is the only way of fixing your friend's problem and you're my only hope of getting back what he took from me. Please, Payne."

Payne swallowed again, his throat as rough and dry as sandpaper. He closed his eyes and hung his head, waging a war against his better judgement. He had promised to find a way of freeing Chica and he had found one. He couldn't give up now when he was so close. But could he do as she was asking?

Could he put aside his hatred of his incubus side and learn to embrace it?

Payne clenched his fists and knew the answer to that question in his heart.

The things he did for his friends.

CHAPTER 3

Elissa had firmly crossed a line and she had a feeling where. She had known from the moment she had set eyes on Payne in the street that he was more than what she could see on the surface. She hadn't expected him to be part vampire though.

Or should that be part incubus?

She should have schooled her features when he had revealed that little titbit about himself, not pointed out that he was a half-breed with some serious issues.

Payne stood before her, his head hung and eyes closed, the soft sandy spikes of his hair catching the firelight and shining. His powerful body was taut beneath his clothes, as tight as a bowstring, his fists clenched at his sides. She could see his struggle written in every toned facet of his physique. He opened his eyes and looked into hers. Their deep grey depths sparkled with flecks of blue and gold, a sign of his incubus nature.

Elissa couldn't imagine what sort of mental number having a dominant vampire side and recessive incubus one did on him. Incubi were in no way submissive creatures. It probably pushed for control all the time, barely held at bay by his stronger vampire instincts. She hadn't been lying when she had said he was all shades of messed up, but she had only meant this war between his dual natures. The way he had reacted said that he had taken it to mean something far deeper than that.

What reason did he have to feel majorly screwed in the head? It had to be more than just the twin species in his genes.

The struggle shone in his beautiful eyes, as clear as day to her. He wasn't bothering to mask his feelings as he waged a silent war in search of an answer to her proposition. The flecks of gold and blue brightened, marking his apprehension but also his desire. He wanted her. She shivered at the knowledge, feeling empowered that such a beautiful man would desire her. She had offered herself to him, wanted him too, but he had denied her.

She had never seen a male so fiercely deny his desires.

She had definitely never seen an incubus refuse an advance from a female.

Normally, they were quick to take what they were offered. She had heard tales about the sexual prowess of incubi from some of the female fae who visited her spell store near the square, every one of them wicked and filling her head with forbidden desire.

She had even met a few incubi, selling them vials of potions designed to remove inhibitions and unleash desires. Ever since the incubi had taken a vow to feed only from willing females, swearing they would never use their abilities to take an unwilling woman and make her sleep with them, she had been busy concocting and selling liquids that would help them bend their own rules.

Payne was nothing like the incubi she had met, and something within her said that it was more than just his dual natures at work.

He gazed off to her left and Elissa took the opportunity to close the purple wooden door, shutting out the noise from the street. She used her magic to lock it. Not that it would stop him from leaving. He could easily teleport away. She did it to drive her point home. She didn't want him to leave. They needed each other.

She ran her gaze over him, starting at his black boots and dark blue jeans, and then drifting upwards to his hands. Strong hands. Long fingers. Made for squeezing, palming, stroking and caressing. She blushed and averted her gaze.

It lingered on his bare right forearm and the scars that littered his skin.

He must have badly injured himself at some point in his life or perhaps his not quite one hundred percent vampire genes meant that he didn't possess the same level of healing that pure vampires had.

Her eyes roamed up his torso. His dark grey shirt fitted snugly to his lithe body, revealing just enough about his physique to arouse her curiosity. The top few buttons were undone, giving a hint of muscled chest and sexy collarbones. No bite marks on his throat. Not into that sort of thing? Maybe he didn't take vampire lovers.

She reached his face and slowed her visual exploration of the six-feet-plus of sex god in front of her. Every feature was sinful, from his profanely sensual lips, with slightly fuller bottom one, to the strong cut of his jaw, to his straight nose and fine eyebrows that flared above his striking grey eyes. They shifted back to her and her breath hitched in her chest. The dark edge to his eyes sent a thrill through her. Mother earth, he was gorgeous.

Forbidden.

She knew the rules. Incubi were demons. Demons were a big no-no for a witch.

She wouldn't break the rules with him. Cross her heart. She just wanted to peel away the layers of this enigmatic male and learn about him. All witches were naturally curious, but Elissa was honest enough with herself to admit that what she felt for Payne went beyond natural.

It was dangerous.

Part of her said that she should help him because he had helped her by saving her from those Rozengard coven brutes. The rest of her said to bargain with him and try to get a taste of him. She wanted to know if the reality would live up to the fantasies she had about being with one of his kind. It was a risk though. A huge one. Incubi were volatile and aggressive. She might end up in over her head and she knew what awaited her if that happened.

Her heart piped up and said to ask only for his assistance. He was her key to getting Luca back. She had sworn to her sister to protect the boy and that bastard had taken him from this very home three weeks ago. She had cried for hours before finding the resolve to get him back somehow.

Elissa had scoured every book in her sister's home but none of them had provided her with a means of finding where Arnaud had taken the boy.

She had been out looking for new books to buy when she had run into the men from Rozengard. They had asked whether she whored herself for demons too, calling her spiteful names and pushing her to get a reaction out of her. She had honestly thought that her life had been about to end in some dank street and that Luca would be lost forever.

And then Payne had come blazing into her life.

When he had caught her wrist to stop her from whipping him, she had seen the markings on his forearm. His lineage. Arnaud had been the second name in. Fate had given her a chance to reach Luca and save him. She needed Payne to help her.

Payne growled. "I'm not interested in playing."

No. He had to help her. She took a step towards him and hesitated when his eyes narrowed on her, bleeding red around the edges of his irises. Volatile and aggressive. She didn't need to provoke him. He had already proven he had a nasty temper.

"Please." If she told him what she wanted to take back from his grandfather, would he help her? Elissa realised that it would only make him more unlikely to lend a hand. He clearly despised his incubus side. He wouldn't want to help another one, not even an innocent child.

He squared up to her and she didn't like the way he towered over her in an obvious attempt to intimidate her. It worked. She wanted to shrink away or at least drop her gaze. It was a struggle to keep her eyes locked on his.

"Tell me what I need to do to know where the incubi den is and I will go alone."

Elissa shook her head. His eyes blazed red. She wasn't going to let him threaten her.

She breezed past him and he huffed. She could feel his gaze tracking her. Her body burned wherever it touched her and she wanted to smile when it slid slowly down her back and settled on her bottom. He so wanted her.

"Tell me, Witch," he barked and Elissa ignored him, going about her business.

She stacked more of the books, taking her time to neaten the piles, aligning the sides of each tome. When she was done with that task, she went to the desk and sorted through the loose sheets of parchment, arranging her new spells into alphabetical order. She wished she had something to knock a vampire-incubus on his backside, but she made her living by mixing politer and more useful potions and so had Verity.

He growled again, this one born of frustration, and Elissa realised that he didn't like it when she acted as though he wasn't a threat to her. It annoyed him. She tested her theory by neatening the glass beakers on the shelves above the desk, ordering them by size from big to small.

He snarled this time, impatient and snappish.

He moved, coming to stand behind her. Elissa didn't look at him. It was hard to ignore her desire to turn and face him. She could feel him close behind her, her body tingling with awareness of his, veins filling with hunger to turn and step into his embrace, tiptoeing to bring her lips to his. Would he kiss her or push her away? She continued to tidy, picking up all her tongs, tweezers, spoons and stirrers and putting them into the desk drawer. She frowned, pausing with her hand on the front of the open drawer.

"Why did you choose the name Payne?" She knew fae kept their real names secret and with good reason. A fae's real name could be used against them. If someone with power used it, the fae would be unable to resist their commands. She focused on the man behind her. He didn't know much about fae or incubi, but she bet he knew about the name thing.

He didn't answer.

Elissa turned to face him. "Don't be shy. You can tell me since we'll be working together."

He glared at her.

She smiled.

His expression only darkened.

Her smile only broadened.

She liked the undercurrent of tension that rippled through him whenever his eyes met hers. Every time they did, the struggle returned, causing lines to bracket his sexy mouth and his eyes to narrow. Oh, he could fight it all he wanted, could fight her all he wanted, but in the end she would win and get her way.

He stepped back and folded his arms across his chest, revealing the lines of his fae markings as they tracked up the underside of his forearms. They curved upwards before disappearing under his shirtsleeves. Where did they go? She wanted to know. Did they snake over his biceps? Did they extend beyond his shoulders? Would he push her away if she traced them with her tongue or moan in pleasure and hold her closer?

That last one shocked her and she forced her eyes away from them.

"Come on, Payne. It's just a silly simple question. I'm sure you can answer it. You're not a dumb blond are you?"

He growled at her, flashing fangs. Elissa barely contained her smile. It was fun to tease him but she was growing tired of this standoff. She walked towards him and he rounded her, going to her desk. He planted his backside against it, crossed his long legs at the ankle and stared at the door.

Oh. A man who knew how to employ the power of the silent treatment. She moved into his line of sight.

He shifted it to above her head.

Freaking curse him. She was tempted but it wouldn't get her anywhere. Incubi were thick-skinned and he would probably punish her by leaving.

Elissa adjusted her plum halter-top to flash a little more cleavage in his direction and then toyed with her long hair.

No reaction. The blue and gold in his eyes didn't even change. His fae markings remained placid cool grey.

It irked her.

Wasn't she pretty enough to get his attention?

She paused.

Did she want him to think she was pretty?

No. She was just bored and annoyed, and he was stubborn. He was a challenge and she liked that. The fact that he was damned hot was just a cherry on top of a very delicious sundae.

He was a way of getting what she wanted. Luca back in her arms, safe and sound.

What she had proposed seemed like a fair exchange to her. She really didn't understand his reluctance. It was strange. He was willing to go alone to get the ring, and might even get Luca for her too if she explained her situation and convinced him that leaving a young boy in the grasp of his grandfather was cruel, regardless of how Payne felt about incubi, but he refused to let her tag along in the role of his lover?

Most incubi would have been all over her, intent on turning it from pretend to real. Payne looked as though he wanted to run a mile from her, as soon as possible and as quickly as he could.

Elissa crossed the room and stopped before him, standing close. He didn't look at her. His gaze remained glued on the strip of wall above the door.

She shook off her nerves and raised her hand. Was she really going to do this? Her fingers shook and she focused, trying to steady them and her trembling heart. She ran her fingertip along his collarbone. No reaction. Her gaze leapt up to his. The colours in them remained muted. He looked like a man waiting for a long jail sentence to end, as though everything depended on surviving until he made it back through that door. Why didn't he just leave then?

Did the ring mean that much to him that he was willing to endure her company and wait until she changed her mind and did things his way?

"Is the 'friend' with a problem your lover?" The thought that she might be caused a weird tight sensation behind Elissa's breastbone and acid in her stomach.

He reacted to that, his gaze darting to her and darkening. "No."

It went back to the door.

It was progress. He didn't have a lover. Elissa found that oddly relieving.

She upped the stakes and ran her finger over his lower lip. He bore his fangs at her but nothing more.

"I don't like strong silent types," she muttered and focused her magic, willing it to reveal the object of his focus.

Her insides lit up.

He was locked on her like a heat-seeking missile on an inferno. She delved a little deeper with her magic, unravelling the threads of his feelings. They were murky. Probably his mixed genes at play. She searched and found a glimmering red ribbon of desire amongst them. He did want her.

There was so much black in his feelings though.

She hoped it was just his genes muddling her spell and not a sign that he held endless darkness and pain inside him. She lowered her hands to his chest, resting her palms against the rock hard muscles hidden beneath his soft grey shirt.

Elissa tiptoed and shivered as their bodies came into contact. She brought her mouth to his ear, making sure their cheeks brushed. His heart thundered like a war drum against her hands and she realised something shocking. He was trembling too. She closed her eyes as he moved, his cheek against hers and his breath cool on her throat. Mother earth, it felt so good that she forgot what she had intended to say.

Her cheek heated against his.

Elissa swallowed and remembered what she had meant to ask him. "Why did you call yourself Payne?"

He grabbed her waist and pushed her away. "It is none of your business. Tell me how to find the incubi den. I desire to leave."

Like hell he did. The remaining trace of her spell said that he wanted to stay. She would have given anything to be powerful enough to cast a telepathy spell on him. Verity had been a witch of that level. Gods, she missed her sister. Unbidden tears sprang into her eyes. Payne released her as though she was about to explode.

"I did not mean to hurt you." He jammed his hands into his pockets.

Elissa scrubbed her eyes with the heels of her palms. "Just something in my eye."

Payne looked away. She had never seen a man look so uncomfortable. She stared at him, trying to figure him out. There had to be a way to make him go along with her plan. She reached out without thinking and absently ran her fingers over the pronounced bumps of the markings running along his right forearm.

He was on her in a flash, his hands grasping her upper arms, claws digging into her flesh. He growled in her face, his fangs enormous and filling her vision. She flinched away, shrinking back and uttering several prayers for protection.

"I only wanted to touch them," she whispered, unable to find the courage to speak any louder.

Payne shoved her hard onto the wooden desk chair. "Don't touch me again. I'm not interested in your fucked up games. I don't like being touched."

Elissa frowned up at him, seeing the truth behind his words in his vivid blue and gold eyes. Red was bleeding into them, mixing with the other colours, subduing them.

"An incubus who doesn't like to be touched?" She found that hard to swallow. She ran her hands over her arms, focusing her magic on them and healing the puncture wounds from his claws.

"I'm a vampire." His low snarling tone warned her to drop it but witches had never been a species who backed off in any situation, even one that could end in blood and death.

She laughed and pointed to his markings. "The writing is there for all to see! A dazzling lineage too... all powerful incubi."

Payne turned on her again, his eyes red now and pupils elliptical. He bore his fangs at her. "I'm a vampire!"

Elissa sighed and curled up on the chair. She really had to stop provoking him. She tried hard to resist but in the end, it slipped out. "Deny it all you want. You are an incubus in part, but you really don't like that part, do you?"

He snarled at her. "Shut the fuck up."

Elissa did hold her tongue this time. His fae markings were black and red. She knew a little about an incubus's markings and those were the colours to watch out for. Anger. Rage. A burning need for violence. Death to anyone who said the wrong thing. She toyed with the nearest spell book, giving him time to cool off so he didn't kill her.

Payne unleashed a low curling growl and shoved away from the desk. He paced across the room behind her and she could sense his eyes on her the whole time, boring into the back of her head. His agitation flowed from him in tangible waves, darkening the atmosphere.

"Just do whatever you need to do to help me." He stalked back across the room.

Elissa's gaze followed him. Was helping him a possibility? He had said that her toying with him and her requests were messed up, but there was something about him that warned he was seriously screwed up in the head.

He shot a glare her way and her eyes darted to the books on the desk. She thumbed through one of them, pretending to look at it while she monitored him, waiting for his temper to fade. The longer she knew Payne, the more she longed to peel away the layers and reveal the man beneath. Could she help him?

She wanted to.

His pacing slowed and he stopped near the large rectangular window. He leaned his forearm against the wall above the window and rested his forehead on it, staring out at the world with his back to her. A sigh raised his shoulders. He didn't feel angry anymore. It was hard to get hold of his emotions but he seemed calm enough for her to approach him now.

Elissa rose to her feet, closed her book, and crossed the room to him. She stopped beside him. His grey gaze slid to her, full of feelings she found impossible to discern.

He leaned back and lowered his arm, towering over her. "What?"

Elissa held her nerve. "What thrills you the most... blood or sex?"

He turned back to the window. "Blood."

Elissa didn't believe that. He seemed to though. He must have worked hard to convince himself. Why? Why not embrace the wicked side of his dual nature?

She opened her mouth to speak but he beat her to it.

In a low, dead voice, he said, "If you don't shut up, then I will make you shut up."

He flexed his fingers and she got the message. She motioned with her right hand, zipping her mouth closed, and then smiled and unzipped it again.

She stared up at him and his eyes shifted to hers, and she was struck again by his masculine beauty and darkness. He radiated danger and even though she knew that she should keep her distance, she couldn't resist her attraction to him. She had to know more about him.

"I swear I will be quiet if you answer one question."

He frowned, eyes narrowing and lips compressing, turning his handsome face as black as his aura. "What?"

"Why do you call yourself Payne?"

He stared down into her eyes and a brief flicker crossed them, a glimmer of darkness, hurt and intense vulnerability. What on earth had happened to this man to make him so wary and make him hate his incubus side? Elissa wanted to ask him that too but it looked as though he wouldn't answer one question, let alone two.

He sighed. "Pain is all I know and all I bring to this world."

Elissa shivered. An overwhelming desire to lay her palm on his sculpted cheek and tell him that couldn't possibly be true raced through her and she barely resisted. The look in his eyes said that he believed it.

He turned away and stared out of the window again, his forehead resting on his arm above it.

She ignored her need to speak and break her promise to be quiet and went to the desk. She sat in the wooden chair and leafed through more of the new books. Payne remained still. The longer he stood there watching the world go by, the less she could concentrate. The words on the pages swam before her eyes and she pinched the bridge of her nose and closed her eyes. What was she doing? She had the method of saving Luca in the room with her. She had to convince him to help her.

Elissa stood, her calves forcing the chair backwards. It scraped across the stone flags, shattering the heavy silence. Payne looked over his shoulder at her, a trace of melancholy in his expression that quickly disappeared.

Had he been thinking about what he had told her and the reason he felt that way?

She wanted to ask him to explain it so she understood why he felt as though he brought only pain to this world but he didn't look as though he would tell her. It was his secret to keep and she had no right to push him to tell her, not when she was keeping secrets from him too.

"I need a walk. Will you walk with me?" She wasn't sure why she asked him to accompany her. Because she feared he would leave if she left him alone here or because she feared the Rozengard males would come after her again?

He nodded but seemed tense. "Where? I don't think it's wise for you to be walking the streets right now... especially with me."

Elissa stifled her smile. He was worried about her. She found that sweet and endearing, a side of Payne she hadn't thought possible.

"Topside," she said. "I like to walk in the woods."

Payne closed his eyes and frowned, and she knew he was focusing through the layers of rock over their heads, trying to sense whether it was daylight or not up there.

"It's dark, gone midnight." Elissa waited for his response. Now that she had thought about the males and he had mentioned them too, the idea of walking alone in the woods unsettled her. She needed air but if those damn Rozengard jerks came at her again, she wouldn't stand a chance against them. Not without Payne at her side. He was strong, powerful. She had never met a male as strong as he was. "Will you walk with me?"

His expression remained dark. "Will you help me get that ring?"

She nodded, knowing that he still meant to go without her to get it. She would just have to change his mind about that. "After I have some air."

Payne nodded too and held his hand out to her. He meant to teleport her. Well, it certainly beat walking but he had snarled and growled at her earlier when she had touched him. Was he that concerned about those males finding her that he was willing to break his no touching rule to get her up to the woods unseen? It was a start.

Elissa slipped her hand into his. Heat chased up her arm as his fingers closed around it. She gasped and stared up into his eyes. The flecks of blue and gold in them brightened, glowing in the low light from the fire and the candles. A louder gasp left her when he pulled her hard against him, wrapped his arms around her, and darkness swallowed the world.

They reappeared in the middle of the grounds of the mansion, the manicured lawn stretching around them and glittering with dew. Elissa shivered, the cold air instantly chilling every inch of exposed skin. She should have put a jacket on before letting him teleport her. She tipped her head back and stared up at the crisp moonless sky above her. Bright stars twinkled and winked at her. She drew in a deep breath and sighed it out, the sight of the universe on display above her relaxing her.

Witches always felt an affinity to nature and whenever she was out in the open, surrounded by greenery, she felt as though she had come home.

Payne moved against her, his arms still around her waist, his cool breath caressing her face. She lowered her eyes and froze as they found his were on her throat. The light from the mansion behind her was weak but enough for her to see where he was looking and that he was thinking very naughty things. She could see his fangs between his sensual lips.

Elissa swallowed her nerves and the action caused him to frown and hold her closer. It seemed he could deny his incubus urges but his vampire ones were more difficult to control. It was definitely his stronger side and that was a problem. She needed his incubus side at the fore, and the only way she could think of bringing it out in him was pleasure. She needed him to give in to his desires. He stared at her throat and the longer he gazed upon it, the faster her breaths came, until she was panting with anticipation in his strong arms.

"Payne?" she whispered, breaking his reverie. His eyes slid to her and the look in them would have knocked her on her backside if he hadn't been holding her so tightly.

A man had never looked at her with such intense desire and need before.

She risked it.

She wriggled her arm free from between them and raised it to his face. The moment she made contact, her palm cupping his left cheek, he sucked in a sharp breath, closed his eyes and leaned into her touch.

He growled. Not in warning this time. It carried unadulterated hunger.

He clutched her closer and her eyes widened, skin flushing with prickly heat. Oh, mother earth. His hardness pressed into her belly and all manner of wanton naughty thoughts cascaded through her mind.

Gods, kiss her.

She needed to be kissed.

He dipped his head, his mouth nearing hers. She couldn't breathe. She slipped her hand around the nape of his neck and tried to make him move quicker.

Payne tore away from her and distanced himself, instantly placing over ten feet of grass between them. He stood with his back to her, shoulders heaving with his breaths. Elissa cursed herself. Too fast. She should have let him set the pace and maybe she might have had that taste of him she so desired.

Craved.

Now she wasn't sure what to say. Things had turned strained between them again. She paced back and forth, her eyes on the stars, searching for inspiration. How could she get him to give up his restraint and unleash that passion on her? She knew it was the key to making him accept his incubus side. He only needed to feel at one with it for long enough to know where to teleport them.

Payne gruffly muttered something and started towards the woods. It seemed their walk was still on the agenda. She had promised to help him get the ring he needed after their walk. Clearly, he wanted to keep his end of the bargain. He was going to be disappointed when she insisted she came with him to the incubi hideout and refused to change her mind.

Elissa fell into line, keeping the ten-foot gap between them. He looked as though he needed the space and she intended to prod a little and try to find out more about him. She liked the thought of a ten-foot lead. If he attacked, she would have the split second she needed to mutter a spell and escape.

"Do you know much about your kind?" She eyed him. No reaction other than jamming hands into jeans pockets. He did that a lot. It reinforced her feeling that he liked to keep to himself and kept everyone at arm's length, if not further, from him.

"Vampires?"

Elissa couldn't find her voice to answer. She shook her head. His expression darkened, giving her the impression that he denied everything about his incubus side, right down to its existence. Why?

What had happened to the male beside her to make him turn on himself?

What had made him hate himself?

Elissa wouldn't stop until she knew.

CHAPTER 4

Payne could feel the questions bubbling inside her and he knew that she wouldn't be able to resist voicing them forever. He wanted her to. She was beautiful, bewitching, and he couldn't deny that he was attracted to her, but whenever she mentioned his incubus side, he wanted to leave and forget helping Andreu and Chica.

He could be their only hope though. Elissa could be their only hope.

They reached the edge of the woods and she paused and faced him.

"Have you ever submitted to someone?"

Payne froze and blinked hard. He had to have heard his petite, enchanting Elissa wrong. She couldn't have just asked what he thought she had. The dark colouring on her cheeks said that she had and was regretting it.

He forced a shrug. "Once or twice."

His stomach clenched. He hoped that answer would satisfy her.

The frown on her face said it hadn't. "I don't believe you've ever really submitted to someone. It isn't in your nature. That's part of your problem... neither side of you can submit. Both sides crave control too much. The incubus and the vampire."

Payne couldn't deny that and he didn't like that she had seen it in him so quickly after meeting him. His version of submission had been letting women go on top. Hers seemed far more threatening, and alluring. Surrendering complete control to a woman? The very thought had him as hard as steel in his jeans but at the same time made him want to flee.

She swallowed, her sexy throat working overtime, and braved a step towards him. Her eyes were dark in the low light but he didn't miss the challenge they issued.

"Submit to me," she said and he almost choked, barely stopped himself from making a scene that would only render him weak in her eyes, stripping him of his masculinity.

He wanted to tell her that there was no way he was going to do such a thing and that he would find some incubi and ask them about finding the den and his grandfather. He still tensed inside whenever he thought about that. The ring he needed was not only in the clutches of an incubus. It was in the grip of his grandfather, a man he had hated without ever knowing.

He must have looked as though he was going to ditch her because she launched forwards and grabbed his wrists.

Elissa looked up into his eyes, that sense of fear, desperation and hope in them again. She needed him.

He needed her, but he couldn't indulge such desires. What she was suggesting was dangerous.

"One night of passion at my command. It will help you. It will help us both. The only way to find the incubi hideout is to embrace your incubus side and let it take control. You'll sense the location and be able to teleport straight there." She paused for air and tightened her grip on him and he could feel her trembling. "Please, Payne. We both need this. Please. Surrender to your desire."

He knew his eyes were positively glowing at the prospect but he couldn't stomach the thought of allowing his incubus side to take dominance over his vampire one. He shook his head.

"You're afraid." She didn't say it in a mocking way but that was how his heart heard it, and he couldn't deny it. It wasn't fear holding him back though.

"It isn't that," he said calmly and her grip on his arms eased. "I cannot do it. My incubus side will want to dominate you as well as the vampire in me."

"That's only because you've never really embraced it. You constantly want to reject it. It's the whole point of the exercise... you need to embrace that side of yourself if we're going to stand a chance of discovering where the other incubi are hiding."

Payne despised how easily she could see through him to the truth he tried so hard to hide. What else could she tell about him whenever she looked at him? He hoped she couldn't see some things, like the black stains on his soul.

"You just want to get into my pants." He gunned for charming even though it was hard to smile at her when his insides were in turmoil, his heart and head tearing him in too many directions.

She smiled and it was dazzling, alluring and just a little bit wicked. He had the feeling that her one night of passion had absolutely nothing to do with helping him connect to his incubus side so he could find this place of the incubi. She really did want him. Why? What did she see in him to make him worthy of her that he couldn't?

He had tried to figure her out back in her temporary home. Whenever she had glanced his way with desire darkening her beautiful eyes, he had tried to understand what it was about him that made her look at him that way. He had snarled at her, gnashed his fangs, and hurt her, and she had still found ways to touch him, still smiled at him, still wanted him.

He didn't understand her at all.

"I'm only asking for one moment with you, Payne."

One moment too many and one thousand too few.

Payne stared at her, knowing his eyes were brightening and unable to stop the reaction. He couldn't take it anymore. He was so hard for her, too far gone to care about the danger or the details. She was offering him a moment with her and he needed it. He had never needed anything so fiercely. She might break him though. He had never submitted to anyone because it wasn't in his nature, but he would try for her, because right now he would do anything for a taste of this exquisite beauty before him.

He would try to stifle his incubus side to protect her. He couldn't embrace it though, not as she wanted.

He had only embraced his incubus side once in his lifetime and it had awakened something terrible within him.

That night, he had lost the only woman he had ever loved.

CHAPTER 5

"One night."

Those two words leaving Payne's lips shocked Elissa. She didn't feel as though she had won. It was offered grudgingly. Still, a single night of pleasure with Payne. It excited her but scared her too. She wasn't sure where to begin or what he would expect from her, or whether she really could help him accept his incubus side so they could discover where the rest of his kind lived.

When she had suggested he submit to her, she had done so because she had figured that she needed to do something dramatic in order to push him over the edge and force him to give in to his needs. It had worked. Now what was she meant to do?

She had asked him to submit to her. She had never done anything like this before. She had never experienced being with a male as strong as Payne was. She'd had mortal males in her lifetime, but nothing that had lasted, and she had never been with a demonic breed of fae because certain aspects of them were forbidden. What was he going to say about that when she told him?

What if he was too powerful for her?

Her heart told her to give up this foolish venture before it ended in tears and disaster, but she couldn't ignore her intense attraction to him or the need that shot through her whenever she looked at him.

Payne excited her. He was forbidden fruit and she was desperate for a taste. She knew that with him she would be pushing the boundaries and dancing with danger. It thrilled her and she couldn't help wanting it. She ached to know a demon's touch.

Payne's touch.

Nerves skittered through her, causing her hands to shake and palms to sweat. They worsened when Payne slipped his arm around her waist, pulled her flush against his body, and teleported them back to her sister's home. She swallowed and tried to stifle her trembling, but the way he frowned at her said that she couldn't hide it from him. Fool. Of course she wouldn't be able to hide her fear from a vampire. They thrived on sensing it in others.

She tipped her chin up, grabbed his hand and led him towards the bedroom.

Mother earth, what was she doing? She didn't have the first clue about this sort of thing. She had never seduced a man, let alone played the role of dominant to their submissive.

They entered the bedroom and she stopped dead, her eyes on the blue satiny sheets covering the double bed. The silver stars stitched onto the material blurred. Her panic increased.

Payne rounded her, his eyes on her chest. Listening to her rushing heart?

"Do you need a moment?" There was a beautiful tilt to his lips, as though he found her nerves pleasing. Why? It struck her that it was because it gave away that this wasn't the sort of thing she normally did with a man.

Elissa shook her head, trying to look casual, and then nodded. His smile widened and he reached up and grazed his thumb across her lower lip, sending a hot shiver through her. He let his hand fall from her face and went back into the main room of the house, closing the door. Very courteous. Giving her privacy to get her explosive nerves under control. She listened, hoping he hadn't just used the opportunity to do a runner. She heard beakers clink together and the curtains close.

She drew a deep breath and exhaled. Gods, she wanted this, wanted him, but what the hell had she just signed up for? He would be expecting sexy. Could she do sexy? Could she be dominant with a man?

Dominant wasn't in her nature.

She squirmed on the spot. Already desire was dampening her knickers. She glanced at her wardrobe. Sexy. She could be sexy for Payne. She wanted to be that way for him.

She pulled out her drawers and dressed in her most provocative black lace underwear. A simple bra and shorts. The mirror hanging on the back of the door mocked her. Not sexy enough. She could fix that. A little magic improved it, changing her dull underwear to a black satin bustier, thong and fishnet stockings, together with thigh-high black stiletto leather boots. Her heart pounded and desire heated her blood as she stared at her reflection. Very fuck me.

She completed her look by twisting her long chestnut hair into a messy knot at the back of her head and kept her black choker on. Anything to draw his attention to her neck. He might be easier to tease into submission if she was playing her best cards. He wanted to bite her. She had seen it in his eyes. She swallowed again. Gods, would he bite her if she let him? If she made him? The thought that he might obey such a command and sink long sharp fangs into her flesh had her thighs quivering.

The floorboards in the other room creaked. Payne was pacing again. Did he feel as nervous as she did? She felt as though she was about to make a terrible mistake but it was too late now to stop herself. She wanted him. Needed this. She nibbled her lower lip and approached the closed door. She opened it a crack and peeked through to the other room and Payne. He looked troubled, his handsome features set in a dark scowl. How did women make men submit?

Her eyes shifted to the silver rope on the desk.

Another shiver bolted through her, hot from the thought of using it on him.

Payne distracted her. He unbuttoned his shirt and removed it, revealing his bare torso as he walked towards her. A good sign, surely? He wanted to do this too.

He turned his back and she tracked his fae markings with her eyes. The line of symbols ran up the underside of his forearms, curved over the outside of his elbows and snaked over his biceps to his shoulders. From there, they ran across the backs of his shoulders and joined above his spine. They followed the line of it down and ended in a diamond above his bottom, between two very sensual dimples.

Elissa had never seen anything so sexy.

She ached to touch them or run her tongue over them. He didn't like it when she touched them though. Would he be angry with her? Elissa frowned. She was approaching this all wrong. He had sworn to submit to her for one night. A submissive didn't get to be angry or pick and choose what she did.

She eased the door open, waved her hand and the silver rope wound around his wrists and up his forearms, binding them together behind his back. He growled and snarled, his fae markings flashing red and black, and turned on the spot. The moment his eyes found her, he fell silent and still, his chest heaving and muscles straining. The symbols inked on his skin flared in new colours, shades of red and dark pink. Gods, he was delicious.

She wanted to touch him.

Elissa slowly approached him, enjoying the way his eyes were taking her in, drifting over her. His pupils dilated, swallowing some of the grey and the sparks of blue and gold. She stopped before him and traced her fingers over his markings, following them up his right biceps and over his shoulder. His breathing accelerated and he strained against the ropes.

"They're enchanted." She smiled up at him. His eyes bore into hers, dark and hungry. "You can't break them."

He tracked her as she moved behind him, the blue and gold in his eyes brightening. Elissa held his gaze and cautiously lowered her mouth to his shoulder. She pressed her lips to the marks there. He closed his eyes and inhaled, his nostrils flaring and the cords in his neck tightening.

Elissa remained behind him and encircled him in her arms, laying her hands against his granite hard chest. She murmured low in her throat, unable to contain the jolt of pleasure that ran through her. Payne groaned and strained against the ropes again, causing every muscle on his torso to tense and delight her. She skimmed her fingers over the taut ridges of his stomach and bravely continued past the erotic dip of his navel, into the soft dusting of sandy hair that led downwards.

Payne sucked his stomach in and tensed.

She trembled and slid her hand into his jeans, cupping the hard, hot length of him through his underwear. He hissed through his teeth and bucked into her palm, thrusting his impressive length against her. Elissa bit her lip. She wanted to see it.

She rounded him and tackled his dark blue jeans, making fast work of his leather belt and the buttons. He didn't tense this time. She glanced up into his eyes, surprised that he was letting her do this. His eyes were pure blue and gold. No wonder he was behaving himself. His incubus was at the fore and was probably enjoying the hunger that beat through her and controlled her actions. He was feeding on her pleasure.

Elissa grabbed his jeans and boxers, and shoved both of them down his thighs. His cock sprang free, hard and dark with need. Gods, he was big. She stroked her fingers down his length from tip to root. He groaned and his hips jerked, thrusting his erection towards her. She curled her fingers around him and he tipped his head back and swallowed, causing his Adam's apple to bob. He groaned through his clenched teeth. She grazed her thumb over the sensitive crown, eliciting a dark growl of pleasure. A hot shiver chased over her and she did it again, his reaction to this bare caress empowering her and giving her the confidence to continue. He was enjoying this. She was too.

She twisted her hand and ran it down his rigid cock to cup his balls in her fingers. She fondled the heavy sac, teasing him, and he tensed, every delicious inch of him going hard. What was she supposed to do now? Payne was at her mercy and the thought of dominating him was becoming more appealing and thrilling with each passing second.

First, she needed him naked. She pushed his jeans and underwear down to his knees, bending over in front of him. He gave a desperate growl and she glanced up at him. Mother earth, he looked ready to devour her as he stared at her bottom. She removed his boots, letting him stare, wriggling her backside to tease him, and then his jeans, and stepped back to appraise her work.

Payne, naked and bound. Delicious.

He raked hot eyes over her, narrowing them on her breasts and hips. His cock bobbed.

Elissa smiled wickedly. She turned her back on him and bent over, ripping a low growl from him. He thrust his hips, his eyes on her backside. Did he want to nestle his cock between her buttocks? Elissa wasn't sure but she wanted it, so she straightened, tottered towards him on her heels, and turned her back to him once more. She leaned her back against his front and writhed up and down, teasing him with the contact. He strained again, struggling to get his arms free of the enchanted rope.

He stopped when she bent forwards, presenting herself to him, and rubbed herself up and down the length of his rigid cock. He stared down at where they touched, a desperate look on his face. It was wrong of her, but that lost, wild look satisfied her. She worked her body against his, feeling herself growing wetter with need. Payne dipped his hips and joined her, thrusting the length of his erection along her, hitting her in all the right places. Gods, she wanted more. She wanted him to touch her, but she didn't want to undo his wrists.

He snarled when she pulled away and fixed her with a glare. Not quite the submissive he had promised he would be. She would have to fix that.

How?

For starters, he definitely shouldn't be towering over her. Someone submitting should be lower than she was. She grabbed his shoulders and shoved him to his knees. He looked shocked and then aroused. His cock pulsed again, eagerly jutting out from sandy curls. He splayed his knees, giving her a better view of his body, and looked up at her. Sweet heavens. She had never seen such a naughty sight.

Her groin throbbed in response and wicked scenarios flooded her mind.

Elissa commanded the rope. It unwound from his forearms but left his wrists bound, and floated over his shoulder to her. She grabbed the end of it and shook as she raised her leg. She wanted to see his body as tight as a bowstring again. Her heart hammered in her throat. She pressed her foot to his chest.

Payne stared up at her, handsome and wild, a dangerous male at her command. It thrilled her. She worked her foot upwards until the pointed toe of her boot was against his chin and she was forcing his head back. Every muscle on his torso tensed and his eyes swirled bright gold and blue, the incubus side he tried so hard to deny shining through.

Elissa grazed the heel of her stiletto down his throat and he groaned. A ripple of pleasure flowed through her and she could feel it in him too. It seemed Payne was enjoying this. She hoped it stayed that way.

She cleared her throat to find her voice and then whispered, "Kiss my boot."

He didn't hesitate. A jolt of pleasure rocked her.

She shoved the tip of her boot under his chin and forced his head back again.

"Look at me," she commanded and he did, his eyes hooded and dark with passion. "You're beautiful... I want to lick you all over and kiss every delicious inch of you. Would you like that?"

His answer was a strained moan.

Elissa lowered her foot and looped the rope around his neck, forming a leash. She tugged it tight and raised it, forcing him to keep his eyes on her. "Do you like my outfit?"

He groaned again. The blue in his eyes was shining now. "I do."

"You have to tell me more than that. What do you want to do with me when you look at me?" She trembled now, excited but nervous about what he might say.

He spoke, his voice low and sultry, feeding her imagination and relaying his desire. "I want to run my hands up the insides of your thighs and spread your legs to reveal you to my eyes. I want to pleasure you until you draw close and then bury my cock in you, pin you to that wall and take you so hard you will never forget this night... and when you've come, I'll take you again and again until you're begging me to stop. I want to ruin you."

Mother earth, was it wrong of her to want this powerful male to do that to her? The thought of Payne stamping his name on her body had her shaking with need, wet with desire to let him do just that. She was on fire inside, burning to know everything he had just detailed.

Elissa breathed hard, struggling to calm herself enough to speak.

"Do you know what I want to do to you?" she whispered and his eyes darkened again, pupils gobbling up his irises. She stared down into his eyes, clutching the rope, towering over him. "I want to use this rope to bind you to the wall, your legs and arms splayed across it, rendering you helpless."

His eyes flashed brightly at that word. She couldn't tell whether the thought of being helpless aroused or disturbed him.

"And when you're helpless." Another bright flash of gold and blue. "I will strip before you and then..." Her cheeks heated but she held it together. "Pleasure myself in front of you, making you watch me... and when you were close to bursting, I would lick your cock and take you into my mouth, bringing you to the very edge... and then I would begin again, touching myself as I lay in the armchair with my legs spread. I would ease my fingers into my body and pretend it was your beautiful cock inside me, making me orgasm."

His cock throbbed and pulsed, and he arched forwards, straining and groaning. Gods. She felt dirty and it felt good. She wanted to do all that to him, but more than that, she wanted to feel his mouth on her flesh. Could she hold off until she had done as she had said, bringing him to the edge, forcing him to accept she was in control?

Elissa had to try.

She crouched before him, her legs splayed, flashing her flimsy underwear at him. She gripped his cock, stroking the silken length of it, teasing the head at times with her thumb. He leaned back, hips shifting, thrusting his cock through the ring of her fingers. She studied his face and focused on his body, trying to sense how close he was. Not close enough. He grunted.

"Silence." That word was loud in the room.

Payne groaned but nodded. It seemed he was getting into it now.

What else could she make him do?

A pearl of seed tipped his cock and he thrust harder. Elissa took her hand away. His eyes snapped open and he snarled at her, baring fangs.

She yanked on the rope, causing it to tighten around his throat, reminding him that she was the one in control. He looked as though he was going to dispute it and then relaxed, a pained edge to his expression. His hard length bobbed and pulsed.

Elissa needed a cloth. She stood and released his rope, turning to go to the bathroom. Payne shot to his feet.

She turned on him with a scowl. "Kneel!"

He dropped to his knees, hitting the stone flags with an audible crack.

The rush of power she felt from his instantly obeying her was better than any spell.

"Wait." She turned away, walked through the bedroom and went into the bathroom.

She grabbed a small white cloth, wetted it, and came back to him. She crouched before him and cleaned his cock. He groaned and tensed, hips thrusting.

Was he that desperate to climax? He was part incubus and they thrived on sexual play and the rush of satisfaction that came with release. Was she hurting him by making him hold off?

She took the cloth away. It seemed almost cruel to do this to him, but he had looked excited at the prospect when she had talked about it.

She stood, backed away from him and then shimmied out of her underwear. A wave of her hand had the armchair shifting across the room and stopping behind her. She seated herself on it and stared at him. He was panting, defined chest heaving with each strained breath. Her pulse raced and she wriggled on the seat, squirming. What would he look like if she went through with this? She wanted to know.

Elissa slowly lifted her leg, revealing herself to his hungry eyes. Rapt didn't cover it. He looked enthralled as she settled her knee over the arm of the chair, exposing herself, and it gave her the courage to continue. She slowly skimmed her fingers down over her stomach and dipped them into her slippery folds. A moan escaped her at the first brush of contact. She stared at Payne, forcing herself to watch him and see what she was doing to him. He frowned, pure pain twisting his expression. She ran her fingers around her clitoris, teasing both herself and him at the same time, sending a hot rush of shivers spreading outwards along her thighs and into her belly. Payne groaned. Elissa moaned right along with him.

She lifted her other leg and lay back in the chair, and eased her fingers down. Payne stared, eyes wide, breathing hard and fast. The muscles of his arms bunched and tensed as he struggled against his bonds. Blue and gold sparked in his eyes, flaring around his enlarged pupils. She moaned and he growled, one of pleasure this time and need.

She knew what he wanted her to do, and she obeyed the silent command.

She slipped her fingers inside and struggled to resist closing her eyes. Payne's cock pulsed, leaping each time she withdrew. He shuffled to face her but remained on his knees. She threw caution and all sense of embarrassment to the wind and thrust her fingers into herself. Another shiver of bliss raced up and down her quivering thighs as she imagined it was Payne inside her, filling her up, taking her hard and fast, deep and rough, as he had promised he would.

Payne groaned. He looked like a man firmly over the edge now.

"Have you been good?" she said, surprised that she had voiced those words and how husky they had sounded.

He nodded eagerly, clearly straining for some sort of pleasure or touching her. Elissa decided it was time to reward his patience and fulfil one of her desires. She wanted to feel his mouth on her flesh. She had wound herself so tightly that she was the one aching for release now.

She stood on shaky legs and approached him. She grabbed his rope leash with her right hand and stepped between his splayed legs.

"Kiss me." She used the leash to pull him closer. He didn't hesitate.

He leaned forwards and kissed her curls and her thighs, teasing her a little with his tongue. Elissa let him have his way, enjoying the attention he lavished upon her, knowing that she would be in control again soon enough. He ran his tongue up her thigh and kissed across the front of her groin. The tip of his tongue dipped between her plush petals. It wasn't enough.

She stepped back, breaking contact, and was surprised that he didn't growl. She rewarded him and herself by raising her right leg and hooking it over his left shoulder. She fed the rope beneath herself and held it in her right hand again.

"I said kiss me." She pulled on the rope, bringing his mouth to her.

Payne was on her in a heartbeat, his mouth feasting on her, tongue delving deeply to tease her. He shifted lower, arching backwards until he was beneath her, licking her from her slick core to her aroused nub. He tasted her so eagerly that she shuddered from his ferocity. A man had never been like this with her, so hungry for her, so wild and desperate. It thrilled her as much as what he was doing. He suckled her and she grasped his hair with her left hand, twisting the sandy spikes in her fingers, holding him against her. She rocked against his face, unable to keep still. Her legs threatened to give out as the pleasure overwhelmed her.

He lowered his mouth and thrust his tongue into her channel, mimicking sex. Elissa stilled above him, moaning with each plunge of his tongue. She glanced down between them, desperate for a glimpse of his cock. She caught sight of it, dark and tipped with a second bead of his seed, a sign that he was enjoying licking and suckling her. Gods, she wanted him inside her.

The markings that ran over his shoulders and down his spine swirled in hues of red but slowly began to turn blue and gold. He licked upwards again and suckled her clitoris. Elissa rocked her hips. His markings all changed colour.

Payne jerked away. No. Elissa tried to tug him back to her using the rope but he growled and she knew it was a warning.

She looked down into his eyes. They shone as brightly as his markings, vivid cerulean and clearest gold.

"You need to be careful." His voice was a low growl of warning drenched in passion and arousal. "If my skin markings change like this, back off and wait until they become muted and the colours of passion again or risk the consequences."

Elissa nodded. A shiver raced down her arms. Part of her feared the consequences he spoke of but the rest of her ached to experience them.

"You need to embrace this side of your nature, Payne," she whispered and stroked his cheek. "It's the whole point of this. Accept the desires running through your blood and your urges. Feed on this. Bathe in the passion, the desire and the need. Take it all."

He groaned and delved between her thighs again. Elissa wasn't prepared for the pleasure and it shot through her, pushing her over the edge. She clutched his hair and cried his name as she climaxed, rocking against his tongue. He dropped lower and lapped at her, and the thought that he wanted to taste her pleasure as it flowed out of her sent her climbing towards her next orgasm.

She tipped her head back and breathed hard.

Take all of me, Payne.

Her body screamed it but her heart couldn't voice the words.

It was too dangerous.

If she wasn't careful, there would be consequences worse than he had threatened.

Consequences that could get her killed like her sister.

CHAPTER 6

Payne was on fire, burning for her, desperate to taste her again.

He kissed her inner left thigh, teasing her down from her climax. Her pleasure rocked him still, mingling with his own, drugging him and making it hard to control his incubus nature. He pressed his teeth to her soft flesh, feeling it quivering and her pulse beating hard against his lips, trying to rouse his more dominant vampire nature in order to suppress his other side.

His fangs didn't lengthen but his incubus instincts did recede a fraction.

It was always hard to suppress his incubus urges with his vampire desires even at the easiest times, like when he was at Vampirerotique and the shows were taking place. Now, it was verging on impossible. His incubus hungers pushed him to keep going, to lick and tease her to a second orgasm so he could feel that intense rush of pleasure flow through him. It forced his vampire side to recede.

He knew that he needed to embrace the incubus part of himself, just as Elissa had said, but he was afraid of what might happen if he did.

She was so tempting. Her taste, her scent, her sweet arousal and the way she had moaned when he licked her, all of it pushed him to do as she was commanding and feed on her sexual energy.

Sexual energy that he had awoken in her.

A blind man could see that she was new to all of this. That was the only reason he was letting her do this with him. If he had discovered that she had done this with other men, he would have pictured her with them each time she touched him and would have lost control, and it wouldn't have been his incubus side in command.

His vampire nature said to possess her and claim her, to make her belong to him.

Submitting to her like this was a way of achieving that. He had spoken the truth to her when he had detailed what he wanted to do to her, but it wasn't his incubus side that wanted it. It was the vampire in him that wanted to spoil her to all others and make her need him as she had never needed another.

Elissa tugged on the rope and Payne obediently stood, his legs aching as his muscles stretched. He loved the way her cheeks flushed and desire heated her eyes whenever he followed a command without a moment's pause. It pleased her. She enjoyed controlling him.

He couldn't deny that he enjoyed it too.

Or that he was waiting for her to take things to the next level.

She looked so damn hot in that outfit, even more so now that she had ditched her knickers. He wanted to take hold of her, force her to bend over and sink his cock into her hot sheath. He wanted to seize control.

It was hard to deny that urge.

Elissa turned her back on him and he groaned under his breath, his gaze raking over every sensual inch of her, following her sexy curves to her bare bottom. She yanked on the rope around his neck and Payne moved, drifting along behind her, staring at her bottom and imagining being inside her, thrusting into her just as he had threatened.

She led him to the bedroom and he raised his eyebrows, intrigued as to what she had planned now. He could hear her nerves in the frantic beat of her heart but he could sense her pleasure too. She was enjoying this, and he was too, but only because she hadn't done anything to push him too far yet. He hoped that it continued that way.

Elissa turned and rounded him, forcing him to turn with her. She pressed her hot palms against his chest and shoved. He fell onto the bed.

"Up," she said and jerked her chin.

Payne obeyed, shuffling further onto the bed, his heart picking up pace now. He wanted to know what came next. His cock slapped his stomach, eagerly putting in its opinion. Hell, he wanted her on him too. His balls ached, tight with the need to find release, and he wasn't sure how much more he could take.

It was uncomfortable with his arms bound behind him. The rope bit into his wrists. The pain only added to his pleasure.

Elissa mounted the bed and straddled his legs. She crawled up the length of him, giving him a breathtaking view of her cleavage. He ground his teeth when she licked up the length of his cock, briefly teasing the crown with her tongue.

"Don't move."

Payne tried hard to obey that order, even when every instinct screamed at him to thrust. She licked him again and fondled his balls, and he couldn't stop himself when she gave them a brief, hard squeeze.

He moved.

Elissa clucked her tongue. "I'll have to punish you for that."

He loved the way she blushed when she said that. It spoiled the dominant effect somewhat but he liked to see her innocence shining through. It only made what she was doing more erotic.

She gently slapped the end of the rope across his chest.

Payne groaned and she frowned. Shocked by the fact that it had thrilled him?

He wasn't. Over the centuries, he had developed a tendency to give himself over to pain and liked to use it to get off. It was safer than allowing himself to feel a softer version of pleasure. He had closed himself off to good feelings and focused on the dark. He could see just how far he had gone now though and it unsettled him, but he couldn't change who he had become.

He wanted to feel her whipping him. He needed the pain.

He moved again. A flicker of something like horror lit her eyes but quickly faded, her expression softening. She pulled the rope out from beneath him and waved a finger at it. It broke in two, leaving him with his wrists bound beneath him and her with a length of silver rope in her hands. She waved her hand again and it broke into two equal lengths.

Elissa folded the two strands in the middle and held that part in her hand, leaving four lengths dangling free. She stared at him, an edge of uncertainty in her eyes, but bravery too, and a touch of passion and arousal.

She brought the four strands of rope down, gently whipping his chest.

It was wrong of him but he ached for more. He wanted her to strike him harder. He moved again, trying to taunt her into it. She had sworn to punish him if he moved. Her eyes narrowed and she struck him again, harder this time. The whip slashed across his chest and then his stomach, reddening his skin. Payne needed more.

She struck again and the makeshift whip caught his cock.

Payne grunted and arched upwards, hissing from how good it had felt.

Elissa's eyes were wide when he opened his.

Shocked.

She would end this game of hers now. He could see it. She would end it now that he was desperate for it to continue.

Her expression lost its stunned edge and she rallied, striking his stomach again, even harder now. He swallowed and moaned, tried to hold them back so she didn't stop. The whip slashed him again, one of the ropes catching the sensitive crown of his erection. He clamped his teeth together and the groan still slipped out, drenched in desire, thick with hunger and pleasure. It was loud and sounded obscene to him.

Elissa blushed.

"Are you bad?"

He nodded. Very. She didn't know how bad.

She struck him again and again, and he relished every blow. He had never craved something like this before. Each time a moan slipped free, Elissa's look changed, slowly altering to curiosity and then desire. She upped the stakes.

She brought the whip down hard on his chest and then leaned over and kissed the marks, soothing his pain. This, he couldn't take. It was too much. His cock strained, feeling her so close to it, her heat coming off her and washing over him. She whipped his stomach and kissed across it, licking away the red marks. He shouldn't enjoy it so much. It was perverse. It was bliss.

He closed his eyes and tipped his head back into the mattress, relishing the bite and the sting, and the sweet reward of her lips on his flesh. He purred inside, ecstasy flowing through his veins, leaving him heavy and compliant, sated but wound tight with need at the same time. He drank in the way whipping him excited and aroused her, and him too. It was a sweet, sickly, drugging feeling.

His cock pulsed, constantly throbbing, painfully hard. Release coiled at the base, the crown so sensitive that the slightest brush of her satin bustier had him close to coming.

She swept her lips along the latest whip mark and he absorbed her pleasure, getting drunk on her desire. He ached for more. He needed more.

He deserved more.

Elissa sat back and he cracked his eyes open, ready to growl at her to make her strike him again. She stared into his eyes, bewitching him, and lightly ran her fingers down the length of his cock, grasped his balls in her hand and tugged them.

Payne couldn't hold back. His release came upon him in a dizzying flash and he shot his seed onto his stomach, every inch of him quivering and straining, hips shallowly thrusting.

Shame blazed a trail in the wake of his climax. The moment he had his breath, he craned his neck, stared at the mess on his stomach and then up into her wide surprised eyes. Her pulse was off the scale. Her expression softened and she lowered the whip.

She frowned. "How long have you felt you deserved to be punished?"

Payne growled at her and twisted his hands beneath his back, trying to break free of his bonds. There was no way he was going to lie here and let her ask that sort of personal shit. That hadn't been part of their agreement.

She stilled him by leaning over and touching his face. His eyes met hers and he bore his fangs, needing her away from him, not wanting to hear what she would say in case it stripped him of his strength and shattered him.

"You can tell me," she whispered, her expression soft and open. Concern and something akin to affection shone in her eyes. "Why do you feel you bring only pain to this world?"

Payne turned his face to his right and stared at the wardrobe there.

She sighed and stroked his left cheek, her touch searing him. Her warm breath skated over his face.

"I won't push you to tell me... but I won't deal pain for your pleasure either. I won't punish you, Payne."

He growled now and the reaction shocked him. Did he really want her to hurt him? Did he really feel as though he deserved pain?

Darkness welled up inside him. He tamped it down and refused to allow the memories to surface, afraid of what might happen if they did. He didn't want to remember his past. He focused on Elissa, using her as an anchor to the present.

She stared down at him, that concern edged with disgust still in her eyes. He had made things awkward between them and he wasn't sure how to take them back to how good things had been just a few minutes ago, before she had discovered he harboured dark needs.

She moved off him and waved her hand, and the rope around his wrists slackened. He pulled his arms out from under him and rubbed his wrists, flexing his fingers to get some blood back into them. Elissa left the bed and the room, returning with the damp cloth she had used on him earlier.

She held it out to him. He swiped it from her and cleaned up the mess on his stomach, and then retreated to the bathroom. He flicked the light on, revealing a dull grey tiled room, and a mirror and vanity unit directly in front of him. He wet the cloth under the tap, and started cleaning himself in earnest.

Payne paused to stare at the red marks that littered his torso.

He felt sick.

What did she think of him now?

He wasn't even sure what he thought about himself. There was something wrong with him. Messed up. She had hit the nail on the head with that one. His right arm throbbed and he dropped the cloth and held it, fighting to stem the flow of pain as it leached from his heart, poisoning him and turning his thoughts black. Payne closed his eyes and struggled against the surge of memories. Tears stung his eyes. He clamped his teeth together so hard they creaked but it didn't stop the darkness from rising within him, tearing him apart inside.

"Payne?" Her soft voice swept around him, warm and gentle, like a lover's caress.

He hadn't heard her enter. She caught him off guard and before he could think about the consequences, he looked over his shoulder at her. Her beautiful silvery eyes softened and her eyebrows furrowed. He could see himself reflected in her eyes and he ached to know what she thought as she looked up at him in silence. What did she think of the lost male standing naked in her bathroom, scored by a whip, broken by his past, his soul stained black with blood?

She lifted her delicate hand and laid it on his cheek, and gently pressed, silently commanding him to turn and face her. He followed without hesitation, coming to stand before her, unable to mask the pain in his heart.

"Do you want to stop? Because I was hoping you would pleasure me again," she whispered and he wondered if he had ever heard sweeter words. They spoke to his soul and soothed his hurt, chasing the darkness from his heart and his mind.

She didn't despise him or think him broken, a male she wanted nothing to do with. She still desired him.

Payne shook his head, slipped his right hand around the nape of her neck and tilted her head back. He dipped his head and kissed her, telling her that he wanted this to continue, whatever this was. He needed to be with her, needed to drown in her and have all of her, starting with this kiss.

She settled her hands on his chest, slanted her head and deepened the kiss, sweeping her tongue along his bottom lip before tangling it with his. Elation crashed through him, bringing bliss in the wake of it that was so strong that it threatened to overwhelm him.

Elissa drew back, a smile on her kiss-swollen lips. "You get that one for free, but the next one you have to work for. Got it?"

Payne nodded. He understood. If he obeyed her, she would reward him with a brief moment in control.

He followed her from the bathroom and she motioned to the bed. He mounted it and lay where he had been before, but this time she didn't bind his wrists with the rope. Letting him have a little freedom? His cock twitched when she crawled onto the bed beside him, already growing hard for her again. He wanted another taste. He wanted to be inside her this time.

She was moist and hot down there, heavenly. He wanted to bury his cock into that tight sheath and ruin her to all other males, just as he had told her.

She wanted to know his incubus side. She would. She wanted him to pleasure her again. He would.

He would pleasure her so hard that she wouldn't be able to walk for a week.

By the time he was done with her, she would be begging him to stay with her forever.

CHAPTER 7

Payne had been wrong. It was beginning to look like he might be the one begging her. She teased his left nipple with her tongue, her command to keep still ringing in his head, taunting him. He had sworn to obey, wanting the bliss of kissing her. It seemed the incubus in him thrived on the thought of her kissing him. He had tasted magic in their first kiss. Was his fae side hungry for another hit of it?

Elissa crawled up his body, her inner thighs brushing his. She had ditched her bustier, revealing breasts that had him itching to touch. Touching wasn't allowed either. She could touch, lick and bite him all she wanted and he had to keep still.

The biting bit had almost pushed him over the edge a few times and he thought she had seen it because she hadn't done it in a while. Perhaps flashing fangs and growling had been enough to warn her that if she kept nipping, he would end up doing some nipping of his own, on her neck, with fangs.

Her hand glided down the length of his rigid cock and he couldn't stop himself then. He bucked against her palm, seeking the delicious friction. She didn't punish him or cluck her tongue. He took that to mean that grinding his hips was allowed. He did it again, closing his eyes, drinking down the intense hit of pleasure that jolted him to his bones.

"Payne," Elissa murmured and he flicked his eyes open and looked into hers.

She moved back and held his gaze as she licked the length of his erection. She was trying to kill him. He groaned and rocked his hips, hungry for more. She rose off him and crawled back up the length of him, and he stilled right down to his breathing as she reached behind her. She grasped his cock and he clutched the bedclothes as she inched down onto the head and slowly took him into her hot sheath, gloving him tightly.

She stopped when the crown hit the furthest point it could go and opened her eyes and looked down at him. She traced patterns on his chest with her fingers, and he almost growled at her. He didn't want teasing. He wanted thrusting. Hot, sweaty, dirty, thrusting.

He inched his hips downwards. She grabbed them.

"No."

He did growl now.

She eased her grip. "I'm in control."

She didn't sound sure so he nodded to reassure her. She hesitated and then looked down at his stomach.

"You can't come."

"I beg your pardon?" He had surely misheard her.

She couldn't possibly be expecting him to make love to her and pull out before climaxing. She had spent the past god knew how long pushing him to the brink. She would be lucky if he could stop himself from flipping her onto her back and fucking her raw.

"I said you can't come." Her voice was small, almost too quiet for him to hear it, and then she lifted her head and spoke clearly. "You can't climax until I let you."

Payne groaned in anguish but his incubus side lit up, excited by the proposition. Dirty little fucker. He had thought that side of him would have been the one to complain about what she wanted from him, not his vampire one. He had never been into this sort of crap. Normally his incubus side hated not being in control.

Funny. It had been purring for her since she had started playing dominant to his submissive.

Payne really hoped it wasn't a mate thing, because that would mean that at some point in this sordid affair, he had started considering the possibility of binding himself to Elissa.

"You don't know what you're asking," he choked out when she moved on him, settling harder on his cock, her slippery heat encasing him.

She smiled very wickedly. "Oh, I know... incubus."

Payne groaned again, already straining, too hot for her. His powers of attraction might not work on her but he was still a slave to them and his nature, and both incubi and vampires made piss-poor submissives. He had done his best so far but he wasn't sure how much more he could take, and what she wanted from him might just push him over the edge and into dangerous territory for them both.

"If you refuse to do this, then I have no choice but to tie you up and gratify myself while you watch, and I will get very imaginative about the methods I use... but I won't touch you or untie you until the moon has risen and set three times. I'll make you watch me the whole time."

Holy hell. His cock pulsed inside her. Was she trying to make him explode right now? The thought of spending three days at her mercy, without her easing his burden by laying her hands or mouth or any part of her on him, all the while teasing him by pleasuring herself, had him burning hotter and hotter. All of him screamed to obey. He could do this. Couldn't he?

"I want you." She shifted on his cock and he clenched the midnight blue satin sheets in his fists, trying to keep control. "But I can't let you have all of me. Understood?"

Too well. "You're cruel. It isn't fair. I need you too."

Fear lit her eyes and she went to dismount. Payne seized her hips and stopped her. Damn, he knew that it was going to be nigh on impossible to stop himself from climaxing but he would do all that he could. He needed a safety net though.

Payne lifted Elissa off him. Disappointment replaced the fear in her eyes.

"I get it." She looked small as she curled up on the bed beside him, a contrast to the woman who had just been playing dom with him.

Payne teleported to his jeans, grabbed the condom from his wallet, and teleported back to the bed, landing hard beside her. He waggled the foil packet at her.

"We can play, Sweetheart, but I won't guarantee I will be able to completely hold off. I can't. I will reach a point of no return and my hunger will take over and demand satisfaction."

She looked wary.

"You've never dealt with an incubus before, have you?" He frowned at her and stroked his hand down his cock, keeping it hard for her. The feel of her juices coating him was enough to have him hard as steel again.

She shook her head.

Payne smiled to reassure her. She was crazy for leaping into this without knowing what would inevitably happen at some point.

"Under the best of circumstances, asking me to do this is like asking me to stop my heart beating. Impossible. This isn't the best of circumstances. This is the worst." He couldn't believe that he was going to say this and he wasn't sure what her reaction would be, but he needed to put it out there. "I haven't been inside a woman in nearly a century."

Her eyes widened, wonderfully startled. "A man?"

He shot that one down with a glare and pink tinted her cheeks again.

"Why?" she whispered and her eyes darted between his, searching them for the reason.

"Just because." He didn't have a reason to give her, not one that wouldn't reinforce what she already felt about him.

Her eyes narrowed and he again had the feeling she was seeing right through him, down to his tainted soul.

"You wanted to erase that part of you. You wanted to make it go away and you couldn't, so you chose to deny your incubus hungers in the hope it would fade away... you really hate it, don't you?"

Too close to the mark. Payne glanced away, settling his eyes on the ceiling. He could feel her staring still, probing and opening wounds that stung. He wanted her to drop the subject and accept what he had said. Some part of him had thought she would be pleased that he hadn't been with a woman this way in a very long time, but he wanted to do this with her.

What the hell did that mean anyway? Was he already too far gone to save himself? That phantom's words still haunted him.

He dropped his gaze to Elissa and the softness of her expression took his breath away. Only one other woman had ever looked at him like that and he didn't want to draw parallels between her and Elissa. It hurt too much.

"We don't have to do this." Her voice was small but he felt as though she had shouted that.

"Oh, little witch, we're doing this." Payne grabbed her hand and wrapped it around his cock, forcing her to stroke. When she began moving her hand, he released her and let her continue, his length hardening for her again.

"Are you doing this just to get the ring for your friend?"

Now wasn't the best time for questions, they broke his concentration and he needed all of it to mentally and physically prepare himself for what Elissa proposed, but he would answer this one.

He looked into her eyes and hid nothing from her, because she looked as though this had stopped being a game for her too and she felt as lost and uncertain as he did.

"No."

A tiny smile curved her lips and she stroked him harder, tearing a groan from his throat that ended on a growl.

He took her hand away.

"I'll do my best to hold back my hunger." He tore the condom packet open, took it out and rolled it onto his cock.

"But that defeats the purpose of this."

Payne felt like asking whether the purpose of this night was ever anything other than her getting into his pants but held his tongue.

"Fine, you'll get your taste of my incubus side, Witch." He grabbed her waist and pulled her onto his body. She straddled his hips and sat back, her heat trapping his cock between their bodies. "But I warn you that if my markings change colour, you have to stop. Promise me."

She swallowed and nodded. When he had warned her about them earlier, he had noticed her curiosity and had known that she wanted to push him too far to see what would happen. This time, he would spell out what awaited her.

"You shove me over the edge, and there is no coming back, and I can't guarantee I won't... I don't want to kill you."

Her eyes shot wide and her fear flowed over him, intoxicating him and drugging him as heavily as her sexual energy did. Message received. He doubted she would risk it now. Curiosity might just kill his kitty.

Elissa rose off him. Payne held his cock, poising it between them, and watched as she sank down onto him. The erotic sight of his erection easing into her, coupled with the breathy gasps of pleasure she unleashed, sent his temperature rocketing again.

She settled on him, her eyes closed in bliss that ran through his veins. His fae markings shifted in hues of red and pink, colours of passion, but already patches of gold and blue tainted it. Elissa opened her eyes and frowned. Payne smoothed his expression to hide his apprehension from her. She went one better, erasing it by rising off him and driving back down again.

"No touching." She swatted his hands.

Payne moved his hands to the sheets and grasped them. He stared at her, lost in her eyes as she rode him, drawing him into her hot wet core. He wanted to do this without the damned condom inhibiting him. He focused on her eyes, drinking her bliss to boost his pleasure, struggling to hold back his desire. He could easily get off on her pleasure alone without the need for him to climax, but he wasn't sure if he could manage it this time. Being inside her, right where he had ached to be from the moment he had set eyes on her, felt too good.

She arched backwards and he slid deeper into her. One of her hands gripped his thigh behind her to steady her and she reached between his legs with the other, rolling and fondling his balls. Was she trying to break him?

He grunted and tensed, fought his desire to thrust. She moaned and rotated her hips, fingers clutching and squeezing his balls, making him think about how she had done that earlier and he had shot his load onto his stomach. His seed rose to his shaft and he bit his tongue, trying to give himself something else to focus on. The pain helped but his vampire healing quickly took it away, and he had to bite harder to restrain himself.

"Payne," she moaned and he grunted again, his fangs lengthening.

He wanted to bite her.

He growled. He wanted it so much that it became a fight between denying his need to come and his need to sink his fangs into her. He hadn't promised not to bite her. He could do that. Not very submissive of him but she was killing him. She quickened her strokes, moaning each time she took him back into her moist heat.

There was a flaw in his plan.

If he bit her, he would definitely come.

He groaned through a tight throat and she pressed her fingers into the ridge below his balls. Mercy. Payne bucked into her, unable to stop himself, and she squeaked out a moan. He liked that. She sounded as far gone as he felt. He thrust hard again, tearing another cry from her.

"Don't come," she said breathlessly. "Touch me."

Payne writhed and moaned beneath her. She was asking too much now. The markings on his forearms were flushed in blue and gold and it was slowly progressing up his arms. Much more of this, and he would have her flat on her back, her legs over his shoulders and her screaming his name.

She grabbed his hand and forced him to comply. Payne stroked her clitoris as she rode his cock. She was so wet, slippery with arousal, desire for him. He stared at her, watching the pleasure flitting across her beautiful face, absorbing all of it and using it to assuage his need to feel pleasure of his own in the form of release.

"More." She threw her head back, beautifully wanton, her breasts thrusting upwards. He wanted to touch those too.

His balls tightened, semen rising again.

He squeezed her clitoris.

Elissa shrieked and jerked forwards, her head hitting his breastbone and hot breath fanning his chest. Her inner walls sweetly clenched him, sucking him deeper into her hot core, luring him into releasing himself. Everything male in him roared, telling him to roll them over and take her. He expected to crumble and do just that, but then she pulled herself up and rewarded him with a slow kiss.

All of him purred in response and she didn't stop him when he settled his hands on her bottom, holding her to him, and kissed her back. Sweet reward.

She sat back on him and his cock ached and throbbed, painfully hard inside her. She lowered her mouth to his chest, kissing and licking, swirling her tongue around his nipples. Payne could scarcely breathe when she moved back, reached behind her and tugged on his balls again. Witch. He swallowed and told himself this brief flash of painful pleasure was enough. She had sworn not to give him pain but she seemed content with it when it came in this form. He was content with it too.

She wriggled on him and fondled his balls, rolling them in her fingers. His cock pulsed but he held back, biting the inside of his cheek to stop himself from coming.

"You need another reward."

He was nodding before she had finished her sentence.

Elissa smiled. "Touch my breasts."

Yes, Ma'am. He was there in a heartbeat, cupping and kneading her breasts, feeling the hot weight of them in his palms. It was easy to shift his focus to them. He thumbed her nipples and then pinched them between his forefinger and thumbs. She groaned and he moaned with her. It wasn't so easy when she did that, tensing around his cock at the same time.

"Touch my..." She tripped on the word and he smiled and lowered his hand but didn't touch her. It seemed his sassy witch had her limits.

"You want me to touch you where?" he said, teasing her.

She blushed and couldn't look at him. Beautiful. She had spent the past few hours dominating him, detailing wicked things she would do to him, and her innocence could still come to the fore and make her cheeks flush. They darkened another shade and he wanted to touch them to feel their heat.

Wanted to bite her to taste her blood.

"Tell me where," he whispered, coaxing her into finding her voice. He wanted to hear her say it and he wasn't going to obey a half-spoken command. "Order me."

Her silvery eyes flicked to his. "Touch my clitoris."

He groaned. He couldn't remember a woman ever saying these sorts of things to him and it was wreaking havoc on his control. He touched her where she had demanded, fingering her clitoris, watching the bliss dance across her face and feeling her quivering around his cock. He pulsed inside her and she moaned, louder this time, the sound deliciously wanton and dirty.

He wanted to feel her without the barrier of the condom. He wanted to possess her as she had possessed him.

Bewitched him.

"Payne," she whispered, a nervous note in her voice. "Your markings."

He knew. Gold and blue. He lifted her off him. "Playtime is over. Touch me."

His voice was hoarse and tight and he hoped that she obeyed. She pulled the condom off and hesitated. He was about to bark an order at her to give him release when she delved her hand between her legs, gathered her warm juices and slathered his cock with them. Payne groaned. Sweet mercy.

Elissa wrapped her hand around his cock. He groaned, closed his eyes and tipped his head back.

"Harder."

She tightened her grip and gave a swift stroke as she moved to kneel over him, one leg between his thighs. She set a quick pace with her right hand, up and down his shaft, beautifully tight and merciless. Her other hand grasped his balls, rolling and fondling, tugging occasionally to add another level of pleasure. Each stroke of her slick hand that rubbed her essence into his flesh almost had him losing control.

Payne tensed and fisted the sheets, every muscle going as rigid as his cock. He grunted and thrust into her hand, unable to stop himself. His hips moved of their own accord, rising to meet her downward strokes.

He opened his eyes and looked down the length of his body to her. Her eyes met his and her stroke faltered. He knew what she saw. His incubus side. His eyes were swirling, vivid blue and gold, and his markings were matching them. He couldn't control the urge to use his charms on her, to make her give him pleasure. His attempts to tamp them down failed and even though he knew that they didn't affect her, he still tried to resist using them on her. She didn't like it when he turned on the charm.

The way her pupils dilated and her strokes hardened said that she might have been lying about not liking it when his incubus side made her see herself doing things with him. He still wasn't sure how that worked. It had to be her magic picking up on his desires rather than his incubus influencing her. Whenever he had given in to it around her, he had been imagining touching her in some way. Not the normal course of events when he used that part of himself to charm women. Normally it was more like releasing pheromones and them reacting to it, not him picturing doing wicked things with her and them seeing it play out in their mind.

"Don't come." She sounded breathless. Was she picking up the images spinning through his head?

He nodded, willing to play her game still because he had discovered he enjoyed the pleasure he received from obeying her and denying himself to satisfy her.

It was a delicious sort of torture.

It thrilled him.

"Elissa," he moaned and she moaned too, the sound increasing the pleasure he felt as she touched him. He forced the back of his head into the mattress and arched, struggling to contain his growing hunger. He wanted to feed. Wanted inside her again.

He imagined that he was buried deep in her hot sheath, her riding him, her chestnut hair tumbling around her shoulders and her eyes bright with desire, her breasts bouncing with each thrust of his cock. He groaned and she moved faster, longer strokes that made him gasp in pleasure, sent bliss flowing through his blood, heating him and sedating him at the same time. More. He needed more.

He pictured himself rolling her over and pumping her, lavishing her breasts with kisses and licks, grasping her hips as he plundered her and ruined her to all other males.

Made her his.

He saw himself sinking his fangs into her breast as he sank his cock into her body.

"Come," she said in a shaky whisper.

A hot rush swept over his thighs and he jerked his hips up and grunted as his seed shot up his shaft and spilled onto his stomach. His legs quivered and stomach trembled, balls tingling as Elissa tugged and squeezed them. Payne had never experienced anything like it, a full body orgasm that had him melting into the bed, shaking all over and barely able to breathe.

Elissa breathed hard too and when he opened his eyes and looked at her, she was visibly trembling and her lower lip was red, worried by her teeth. She smelled aroused, on the verge of release herself. She frowned at him, hunger in every line of her face.

She looked as though she was struggling for control.

"You were right. Your incubus side is dangerous," she whispered and sat back, releasing his softening cock. She pressed her hand to her chest. Her heartbeat thundered in his ears. "Is it always like that?"

"You saw what I was thinking... my desires?" Payne held her gaze and she nodded. He shook his head and lied through his teeth. "I think it's a witch thing."

She seemed to accept that answer.

It was easier than telling her the truth.

He had thought he had found his mate once, because he hadn't been able to control her fully and his incubus influence had been dampened somehow. Now he knew that he had been wrong.

He stared at Elissa. Beautiful. Enchanting. Bewitching.

Beyond his control and influence.

What she saw in her mind whenever he thought about making love to her was the result of a connection between them.

A bond.

She was his mate.

But would a beautiful witch like her ever want an abomination like him?

CHAPTER 8

Elissa stood in the middle of the cramped shower cubicle, hot water cascading down her bare body and soapy suds following the wake of the sponge gently circling along her right arm. Bliss. The fact that the water was hot and cleansing had nothing to do with that feeling running through her though. The source of it was the part-incubus vampire standing behind her, lavishing her with attention by washing her.

It had been his idea too.

Her mind turned over everything she had already learned about Payne. He was a man who tried to hide everything about himself from the world but he wasn't doing a very good job of it around her. Elissa liked that. He had said that he hadn't indulged in intercourse in a very long time and that had pleased her, but it had also filled her mind with more questions and they were eating away at her. She wanted to know why the man behind her, pressing his delicious firm body into her back, his penis nestled against her backside, hated part of himself.

There had to be a reason.

Elissa took the sponge from him, turned and applied it to his chest, working in circles to clean him. He sighed and she had the feeling he had never done this before either. She would have thought that an incubus would have experienced a shower with a woman before. It was probably high on their list of places to have sex with their conquests.

He was tense beneath the sponge.

Elissa gave him time, slowly easing away his tension and using the opportunity to learn more about his body. She couldn't resist working her way behind him so she could see his fae markings again. They shimmered cool grey and blue with accents of purple. She didn't know that one.

"Contentment?" she murmured as she stroked her fingers down the symbols on his spine and froze when she realised she had said it aloud.

"Something like that." Payne's deep voice was loud in the tiny cubicle. She couldn't believe that he had answered and hadn't tried to pull away from her or stop her from touching him.

Was he enjoying it?

She continued to clean his back, gaze following the suds as they coursed over his muscles. Would he answer more questions?

"Why do you deny your incubus nature?" she said, tense from head to toe and afraid he might turn on her now.

He didn't.

"I used to enjoy and indulge that part of me but I grew weary of it." He braced his hands against the tiles and hung his head forwards. The jet sprayed against his back, showering her in fine mist. She settled her hands on his back to reassure and comfort him. The markings had remained the same colour as before but she watched them, monitoring them for a change. "I no longer gain excitement from seducing women or using my powers. It feels as though women only desire me because of the out of control incubus part."

Elissa felt sorry for him. "It must have been difficult for you to live in a world of vampires when you have fae blood in your veins."

Payne tensed and his markings shifted to reveal patches of black and red. She knew that one. She slipped her arms around his chest and pulled him away from the wall, coaxing him into standing again. She grabbed the shampoo, squeezed a dollop onto her hand and tiptoed to work it into his messy dirty blond hair.

"You don't have to talk about it." She massaged his scalp with her fingers and he lowered himself so she could reach him more easily. She smiled at that. It seemed he enjoyed being fussed like this.

"I almost left the vampire world once."

Elissa frowned at that. "Why? You seem to prefer your vampire side to your incubus one."

She worked lower, scrubbing the shorter hair at the back of his head.

"I had a mate once."

She froze and stared at the back of his head, her fingers paused against his scalp. Oh. She wasn't quite sure how to feel about that. This was just a one night deal. Wasn't it?

Did she want more from Payne than one night?

"Why did you stop?" he said and when she didn't answer, he turned to face her, rising to his full height. His eyebrows knit together, causing his dark grey eyes to narrow, and he looked as though he wanted to smooth his palm across her cheek to reassure her. He ducked his head under the water instead. "I had a mate once but it only lasted a brief time. She was beautiful and I loved her... but she didn't like my vampire nature."

"She didn't love all of you?" She couldn't contain that one.

What sort of woman would love only part of Payne?

He ran his hands over his hair, slicking it back and shook his head. "She was fae and you know what they can be like."

"She thought you were tainted by darkness because you were a vampire." Elissa knew all about fae and their stupid rules. They were worse than witches. Fae had a rule about everything, especially vampires. They hated them more than witches did. At least witches had a reason to find vampires dark and objectionable.

As far as Elissa knew, vampires had never tried to exterminate any of the fae species.

"She wanted me to turn my back on that part of myself and my family... and she almost convinced me to go along with it, but I don't feel I belong in the fae world. I'm closer to my vampire roots than my fae ones, despite all the shit that has happened to me."

"What happened?"

He sighed and leaned his shoulders back against the tiles. "I asked her to love me as I was, a vampire first and foremost."

Elissa knew from the pain surfacing in his eyes that it hadn't ended there and it hadn't ended well.

Payne closed his eyes and his markings shifted again, turning shades of black, purple and blue. Was that hurt?

"What did she do to you, Payne?" Elissa laid her hand on his cheek and he opened his eyes and looked down into hers. Red edged his irises but he still looked lost and wounded.

"She knew my real name."

"Mother earth! She didn't?" Elissa couldn't contain her shock. Her heart went out to him and she had her arms wrapped around his neck before she could even think about what she was doing. He surprised her by looping his around her waist and crushing her against his body. He was trembling.

He turned his head and settled his cheek on her shoulder. His voice dropped to a low, hoarse, wounded whisper that conveyed the terrible depth of the pain in his heart. "I hated her... I hate her."

He growled and Elissa tightened her grip on him with one arm and stroked his back with her other hand, hoping to soothe him. His fingers pressed hard into her lower back, clutching her to him so desperately that she wanted to cry for his sake, because she knew that he was crying inside, wounded beyond repair by the woman he had loved.

She had tried to use his name to enslave him.

Mother earth, no wonder he had been so reluctant to submit to her tonight.

No wonder he was so messed up about his dual nature.

She lowered her head and kissed his strong shoulder, pouring her heart into each press of her lips, wishing they would take away some of his pain and his suffering.

If she had known what that bitch had done to him, she never would have asked him to submit to her. She would have done things differently.

Elissa held him, feeling him shaking in her arms. How could someone who had claimed to love him do something so terrible to him? The woman must have known that Payne was at war with himself, unable to accept his fae blood for some reason. Yet she had tried to make him reject his vampire side, the one part of himself he was comfortable with.

What his mate had done to him was abominable and inexcusable, but Elissa knew it wasn't the reason he felt he brought only pain to this world. Had something even more terrible happened to him in his past?

"You're getting cold," she whispered against his damp shoulder and turned off the water. "Can I ask you something and will you answer honestly?"

He drew back enough to rub his face but not enough that she could see what he was doing. Had she made him cry by bringing up his past? The thought that she might have made her feel abysmal. He cleared his throat and stood, no trace of tears in his eyes.

"Go ahead," he said, sounding composed and emotionless. His markings were dull grey again. She was beginning to get the impression he could school them as easily as he schooled his features.

"Why did you agree to do this with me?" She had never felt so nervous about posing a question. She stood before him, naked and shivering, afraid that he would tell her he had done it to further his connection to his inner incubus so he could get the ring.

He smiled and her heart missed a beat. "Because I wanted you. Simple as that. You're beautiful."

Those words warmed her but couldn't fully chase away the chill gradually stealing into her soul. She smiled and took his hand, and led him from the shower.

"Why did you want to do this with me?" he said and she looked over her shoulder at him, and then raked her gaze over his gorgeous body. Did he really need to ask?

She smiled properly.

"Because I wanted to get into your pants."

He grinned and gave her a look that said he had known her reason all along.

She tossed a towel at him and dried herself off. When she was done and he had finished too, she took hold of his hand again, her nerves returning. This was probably going to be one step too far but she was chilly from the shower and sharing body heat sounded like a really great idea to her.

She led Payne to the bed and drew the dark covers back. Payne smacked her backside and she gasped.

"I get the right side."

She frowned at him. He was calling a side of the bed? Someone had certainly made himself comfortable in her home. She realised that the right side of the bed meant he would have to walk around it. She could go along with that.

He set off and Elissa stood there, barely resisting her need to sigh as she watched his cute behind as he walked. The man did have the body of a god. A sex god. Purr.

He hopped onto the bed, reached over and grabbed her arm, pulling her down onto it with him. He threw the covers over them both and kissed her breathless.

"You think this will work?" he said and lay back, dragging her with him.

Elissa settled into his side, her head on his chest and his right arm around her. She hooked her right leg over both of his and placed her hand on his chest. His heart was thumping. She smiled. She had enjoyed that kiss too. It had felt different to the passionate ones they had shared in the heat of the moment.

"We'll find out soon enough." She closed her eyes and listened to his steady heart. Strong. Powerful. Just like the rest of him.

That kiss had felt too good.

Elissa focused on Payne. Being held like this by him felt too good too.

She wasn't sure what she was going to do now.

This had started out as a game, a way of satisfying her curiosity about him, but she could see now that she was attracted to him, and that was a dangerous thing.

She'd had her one night with him.

Her head said to explain to him about Luca in the morning and let him go alone to retrieve the boy and the ring from Arnaud.

Her heart said to go with him and relish every second that she had with him, no matter how dangerous it was to allow herself to fall for him.

Elissa looked up at him, watching him sleeping, his face soft and relaxed. Beautiful.

She was already in too deep to walk away.

She wanted to be with Payne.

Even if it meant dancing with danger.

Even if it meant risking ruin and death.

CHAPTER 9

Payne woke alone with the fall of darkness, deeply sated and a little sore. He stretched out beneath the blue satin sheets and settled his hands behind his head, unable to remember the last time he had woken feeling so relaxed or the last time he had slept through the day like the dead.

Normally he woke several times in the daylight hours.

He hadn't stirred once while Elissa had been tucked against his side, warming him with her soft body, her palm resting on the centre of his chest and her breath skating over his skin. He had fallen asleep to the sound of her steady heartbeat, counting each one, thinking about everything they had done and the things he had confessed. What did she think of him now?

There had been sympathy in her silvery eyes, and she had held him so close to her, tighter than anyone had held him in his long weary life. The feel of her arms around him, and the warm emotions flowing through her, had stripped away his strength and left him shaking right down to his bones. He had wanted to stay there with her in that shower, resting on her shoulder, letting her compassion wash over him and carry away the pain. He had wanted to forget it all in her arms, hoping to find a way to reinvent himself as something better, something she would look at with affection rather than pity.

The sound of a page flipping came from the other room. Elissa. Leafing through her books. When had she risen?

Had she kissed him while he slept before leaving him alone?

He shook his head at that question. Dangerous thoughts. She had gotten under his skin too quickly and he knew better than to believe there was a happy ending in the cards for them.

Look how well it had turned out the last time he had thought he had found his true mate.

Payne sighed and shook those dark thoughts away as well as the lighter thoughts of Elissa that were just as deadly and just as likely to cause him pain, focusing on his inner incubus instead. He couldn't remember ever wanting to feel it, not like this. He had never intentionally called it to the fore for no reason other than to feel it within him.

Part of him.

It was quick to come out of hiding, dominating his vampire nature and subduing it. His thoughts drifted to Elissa and the things they had done, and the things he wanted to do with her. He wanted to be in control this time. He wanted to finish inside her, claiming her body as his. He would make her scream his name as she climaxed and would feed on the intense pleasure that flowed through her in the wake of it.

It was too much.

His cock tented the blue material covering his body and he groaned.

Payne denied the urge to stroke himself and drew his hands out from behind his head. He raised his arms in front of him and stared at the fae markings. They swirled in shades of gold and blue. His incubus nature was in control now and he didn't feel as he normally did when it happened. Rather than anger and disgust, he felt calm and still in command. The shifting colours mesmerised him and he lost himself in them, his vision blurring.

A weird sensation grew in the pit of his chest. A hot tingling that brought a strange notion with it.

It was as intangible as smoke but he felt it.

He knew where to go.

Payne teleported out of the bed and into the room with Elissa.

A woman passing by on the dimly lit street outside the window gasped. Payne cupped himself. She hurried away.

"Are you insane?" Elissa rose from the chair and hurried to the window. She tugged the dark curtains closed. Payne felt like mentioning she was the one who had opened the curtains even though he was sleeping nude in the next room.

He grabbed his underwear and slipped it on, quickly following it with his dark blue jeans. A flicker of disappointment lit Elissa's eyes when he donned his dark grey shirt. Had she been expecting an encore? That had him stiff in his jeans. Later.

"It's time to go." He began buttoning his shirt and Elissa's gaze dropped to his torso.

"It worked?" Her cheeks heated. Damn, he wanted her when she looked so innocent. It was hard to deny the urge to take her first and then head out, but he needed to do this before he lost his nerve.

He nodded.

Elissa packed some things into a black leather satchel, and then rushed past him into the bedroom. She shed her dark red robe, revealing lush bare curves. Payne couldn't stop himself then.

He teleported right behind her and stepped into her. He swept his hands over her hips and drew her backside against his crotch. She stilled in his arms, her breathing rapid and heart racing. He lowered his head and pressed kisses along the subtle curve of her shoulder. Her breathing hitched when he gathered the waves of her chestnut hair and swept it over her other shoulder, away from her throat.

Payne licked her neck, his fangs lengthening.

He wanted to taste her.

She twisted in his arms, coming to face him. "What are you doing?"

Payne stared at her neck, unable to tear his gaze away from the smooth creamy column that tempted him more than anything, more than her naked body wrapped around his again. "Tasting you."

She shook her head and he frowned. "No tasting. No biting. We don't have time for this."

Her nerves flowed through him, carried by her scent and her touch, and sounding in the tremulous beat of her heart.

"It won't hurt," he whispered, his eyes glued to the flickering pulse on her throat. He would make sure it was pleasurable for her, and for him. He couldn't remember the last time he had taken blood from someone he had been intimate with, but it had been a very long time ago, and he couldn't deny his need to do this, to have her in all the ways imaginable, slaking the needs of both sides of him. He had assuaged his incubus desires. Now he had to tend to his vampire ones. "I'm hungry. You made me hungry."

His gaze darted to hers. She looked torn between refusing and accepting. He could see the war happening behind her soulful silvery eyes. Part of her wanted this, hungered to know his bite as fiercely as he hungered to know her blood. He only had to work on that part of her, cranking it up until she couldn't say no.

"If you bite me, it might look suspicious." She sounded too breathless to believe that. It was a piss-poor excuse.

"Why?" He pulled her closer and her eyes widened, her pupils dilating. "They'll know I'm part vampire the second I set foot in their den. You're supposed to be my lover... a vampire's lover would have bite marks."

She fell silent, staring into his eyes, the black chasm of her pupils swallowing the colour in her irises and turning them dark with need.

The tiniest sideward shift of her chin was all the invite he needed.

Payne dropped his lips to her throat, feeling her pulse flickering wildly against them, and inhaled her sweet scent. Saliva pooled in his mouth and his fangs stretched long, hungry for a taste of her. He would have it.

He opened his mouth and eased his fangs into her flesh.

She moaned hotly into his ear, her reaction sweet and intoxicating him. Payne closed his eyes, eased his fangs out and gave a shallow pull on her blood. It flooded his mouth, hot and heady, scorching him with its intensity. He had never tasted anything like Elissa. He could taste the magic in her veins, tinny but strong with a sharp edge. His body reacted to the blissful taste of her in an instant, cock as hard as steel against his tight jeans, the pleasure of her blood flowing into him obliterating the pain he should have felt. He sank his fangs back into her, deeper this time, unable to resist his need to mark her for all to see.

Payne moaned against her and drank deeply of her sweet blood.

Elissa clung to his upper arms, her fingertips pressing into his flesh, short nails digging through his shirtsleeves. Payne clutched her bare bottom and ground his erection against her stomach, aching to be inside her in every way possible.

"We really don't have time for that." She sounded breathless and as intoxicated as he felt. "If you start that again, I won't want to stop for hours."

That drew a smile from him. Blood spilled from the corners of his lips and he closed them over the wound and sucked again. She moaned, the sound wanton and delicious. The scent of her arousal drove him to take things further with her and satisfy both of their desires, but she was right. If they got down and dirty again, they would be at it for hours. He fully intended to drive her mad with pleasure next time.

"We can play again when we're at the incubi compound." There was a hopeful edge to those words.

Payne groaned in agreement, strangely pleased that she still wanted him after everything he had already revealed to her.

The thought of taking her again caused his incubus side to flare into life. He drew pleasure from the vision floating around his mind as well as the taste of her blood as it flowed into him. Ecstasy. He had found Heaven.

The vampire side of his nature said to bite her harder.

Payne forced himself to withdraw and swiped his tongue across the bite mark to seal the puncture wounds. He wasn't going to hurt her. Not Elissa.

He licked the rivulets of crimson from her bare chest, cleaning her up and savouring this all too brief moment of contact with her. He ran his tongue around her pert left nipple and she moaned, the sound breathy and wanton, filled with hunger that he wanted to satisfy. She clung to him still but the pressure of her grip was already easing and her heartbeat was steadying.

Payne set her away from him and stepped back. Pink flushed her cheeks and her pupils blotted out most of her silvery irises, her desire there for him to see as well as smell on her. It was hard to resist his urge to grab her, drag her back into his arms, and kiss her until she surrendered to him. Her gaze flickered around the room, occasionally falling on him, her air hesitant now, edged with awkwardness that brought a smile to his face. She didn't have to be ashamed that she had enjoyed his bite. It pleased him.

He swept his fingers through his sandy hair, preening it back. Elissa's eyes met his, she blushed again and then turned, walking on wobbly legs to the bathroom. Payne forced himself to turn away from temptation too. He adjusted the rock-hard erection in his jeans and focused on mundane things to make it go away as he walked stiffly into the main room of the house. He finished buttoning his shirt and then pulled on his socks and rammed his feet into his boots and tied the laces. He arranged the hems of his jeans over them and then sat in the wooden chair beside the desk. The spell book Elissa had been reading was still open. He glanced at the page.

A cloaking spell.

He looked closer. Not the sort that hid someone from others but the type that hid something about someone. Something specific.

What did Elissa want to hide from everyone?

She came out of the bedroom and paused at the threshold. Payne eased back in the chair and she wiped the nervous expression from her face. It didn't hide the emotion behind it from his senses. Why did the fact that he had noticed the spell scare her?

Elissa grabbed the satchel and his gaze roamed over her as she slung the black leather strap over her shoulder. She had dressed provocatively again, pairing dark blue jeans with a black halter-top. Again, no bra. The black material gathered under her breasts and flowed from there. Pale pink stars decorated the hem.

"Not on duty?" he said and she quickly shook her head. So, whatever she had lost and wanted to regain was a personal matter. Interesting. "You know what my grandfather looks like?"

Payne had almost choked on that word. Grandfather. Bastard. He would be lucky if Payne could control his urge to rip him apart with claw and fang. He wanted him dead, but he couldn't kill him until he had what he needed.

She nodded.

His eyes narrowed on her. "Does he know what you look like?"

She shook her head and Payne didn't believe her. If she was lying, his grandfather might recognise her and bolt, and Payne would never get the ring for Chica and Andreu.

Payne stood and held her gaze, giving her a moment to amend her answer. She didn't. He held his hand out to her and she slipped hers into it. The warmth and softness of her hand had heat coursing up his arm and through his blood. He pulled her against him, wrapped her in his arms, and stared down into her eyes. She looked as nervous as he felt. What did an incubi den look like? He really did hate going blind into a situation. Was he about to teleport Elissa into a nest of vipers who would all be out to get a taste of her?

He pulled her closer. He wouldn't let them have her. Elissa was his.

He focused on the feeling in his chest and teleported.

They landed in the middle of the moonlit gravel drive of a very beautiful Georgian manor house. Elissa shifted in his arms, rubbing against him in a way that had him gritting his teeth and struggling to focus.

"The whole area is cloaked," she said and he looked down at her. She glanced up at him, her eyes briefly meeting his before she scanned the area again. "It's a powerful concealment spell. No wonder only incubi can find this place. I wouldn't be surprised if we haven't just popped off the grid completely."

Interesting. Did that mean that to her kind, she had just disappeared? It was certainly a convenient spell for the incubi to employ. No one would notice if an incubus accidently killed their host here. That person would just look as though they had gone missing, never to return, and those looking for them would never find a trace of them. Payne didn't want to imagine how many lives had ended in this place, or how many bodies the elegant grounds now concealed.

His senses sharpened, eyes assessing his surroundings as he put all of it to memory and searched for a sign of trouble. The first thing that Payne's sensitive hearing picked up was the continual hum of moans coming from the house. His incubus side flared up again, lured to the surface by the sexual energy crashing over him. He had never experienced something so intense. It pressed down on him, urging him into surrendering to his sexual desires, goading him into sucking down the pleasure and getting high on it. His knees threatened to weaken. They trembled.

He trembled.

Payne growled, crushed Elissa to his chest and ground his erection against her belly. She stared up at him through wide wild eyes.

"Payne, your eyes are glow—"

Payne cut her off with a hard, aggressive kiss. He dominated her mouth, forcing her to open for him and thrusting his tongue past the barrier of her teeth. She wriggled in his arms, rubbing against his cock. He growled again, hunger tearing through him, driving him to obey his instincts to feed from the female in his arms. He needed to get inside her. He needed to fuck. He teleported and reappeared closer to the mansion. Elissa grunted when he slammed her back against the wall and pinned her there, trapping her body with his, caging her in his arms. He mastered her mouth, not giving her a chance to draw breath, desperate to drink down her pleasure and spark more within her.

She pressed her hands against his chest.

Something slammed into him, hot and fierce, sending him flying backwards through the air. He landed hard, spraying gravel in all directions and rolling. His arm twisted beneath him, pain shooting outwards from his shoulder, and he growled as he finally halted on the driveway. Sharp hot pulses beat through his bones, dampening the hunger that had spiralled out of control within him, giving him a chance to claw back some semblance of sanity.

"Elissa," he gritted out and slowly pushed himself into a position where he could check on Elissa, fearing he had hurt her and needing to see with his own eyes that he hadn't.

Elissa stood with her back pressed against the wall, breathing hard, fear coming off her in strong waves. He battled his urges, struggling to get them locked down, not wanting her to fear him or hate him, and not wanting to hurt her. He would if he lost control again. He had never been around other incubi and he swore he would never go near them again if he made it through this because he didn't like how it made him feel. It triggered something within him, pushing him dangerously close to the edge.

"Maybe this was a bad idea," she whispered.

He struggled to subdue his hunger for her. "I think we need to get in and out as quickly as possible."

That had to be the first time he had ever said something like that. Normally, he liked to take his time about things, drawing them out. He grinned to himself, wicked thoughts spiralling through his mind and lust fogging his senses. Gods, he wanted Elissa naked and bucking beneath him. He would make it last all night and she would be weeping, begging for release before he finally gave it to her.

She nodded and it took him a moment to clear his head enough to remember what they had been talking about. In and out. He grinned again, dirty thoughts crashing back into his head. He managed to shove them out before they got comfortable this time and pushed onto his feet. His head spun. What had she hit him with? Whatever spell it had been, he had deserved it. He blinked and gave the world a moment to stop dancing before his eyes. Elissa approached him and he held his hand up, warning her to give him a minute. He still hadn't got his hunger in check. If she laid a hand on him, he would have her back in his arms and breathless again, or worse. He had no qualms about public sex or inclement weather. He would take her right on the drive.

"You okay?" she said in a voice laced with concern and he blew out his breath and nodded.

"Ready." As he ever could be. What he was about to walk in on was going to tip him over the edge again, he knew it, but he had to go in there and get that ring.

He kept some distance between him and Elissa as they approached the manor. The door was open a crack. Evidently, incubi didn't worry about intruders. Hell, they probably welcomed them to the party. Anyone who had come here had probably been lured by the sexual pheromones the gathered incubi were throwing off. Willing hosts for the males inside. He pushed the heavy wooden door open and stepped into the building, Elissa trailing behind him.

Payne stopped dead and Elissa bumped into his back.

He had thought that the erotic acts he witnessed on the stage of Vampirerotique were hard to handle. He had been mistaken.

The orgy happening right on the pale marble floor of the elegant vestibule of the mansion was the epitome of hard to handle.

He tried not to stare, and not only because the incubus in him was loving it and he had a sick urge to strip off, join in and reap the rewards. He didn't want the sight of seven naked males tangled with what looked like at least twelve females seared onto his eyeballs.

Elissa gasped. One of the men looked at her, his blue and gold eyes shining brightly, his smile wicked. Elissa took a step towards him.

Payne realised he had overlooked something critical and it royally pissed him off. The males here could lure and control Elissa. Over his dead body.

Payne roared at the male and grabbed Elissa, pulling her into his arms and tucking her against his side. She still tried to get to the man, wriggling against Payne and elbowing him. Payne turned his snarl on her and her eyes darted to his. Shocked didn't cover the horror in her eyes.

A dark-haired male approached from a corridor on Payne's left, this one actually dressed, wearing a smart dark grey suit. "Can I help you?"

The male's swirling eyes dropped to Payne's arm around Elissa and he raised his eyebrows at Payne's markings visible beyond the rolled up sleeves of his shirt.

"I want to see him." Payne knew without a doubt that the man would know exactly who he was talking about.

The man nodded and waved his arm towards the corridor he had come from, a smile plastered on his face. Payne kept Elissa close to him and followed the male, his senses on high alert, tracking every other male in the room. If they looked at her, he would kill them all.

They walked down a long red and gold corridor. There were no paintings on the wall on his right but dark stains marked where some had hung in the past. The windows on Payne's left revealed the lamp-lit gardens. Elissa trembled against him. Payne squeezed her shoulders and she lifted her eyes to his. He smiled, wanting to comfort her and reassure her that she was safe even when he wasn't sure whether that word was applicable to either of them. What the hell had possessed him to agree to come to this place? The distance between him and the orgy was growing, but his dark sexual hungers weren't lessening. They roared within him, fiercer than ever, driving him to take Elissa and teleport them somewhere private.

Or forget the private and the teleporting part, and just take her right here and right now, regardless of their company.

The male opened a door on his right and disappeared into a room. Payne struggled with his incubus hungers, trying to get a lid on them, and peered into the pale blue room. It looked much like a library or a study, with bookcases lining the walls. Some of them even had books, although they looked as though someone had tossed them onto the shelves, uncaring of how they landed. A large oil painting hung above the fireplace directly in front of Payne. The smoke from the fire must have damaged it over the ages, clouding the image depicted on the canvas. He couldn't make out the landscape.

Payne entered with Elissa tucked close to his side. The man swept his hand towards the deep blue couches encircling the fireplace.

"Do sit. I will be but a minute." The man disappeared.

"What the freaking heck are you doing?" Elissa hissed.

"I need his scent and since you said that my grandfather had never met you, I figured it would be safe to meet him. Believe me, Sweetheart, I want nothing to do with the son of a bitch. As soon as I have his scent, we can find his room in the mansion, get what we came here for and get the fuck out."

"I lied."

Payne groaned. Why did his instincts have to have been right about that? He looked around the lushly furnished room, searching for a place where she could hide while he got a whiff of his grandfather. He needed somewhere safe, away from other incubi. They were near the end of the mansion, far from all the fucking, but it still set him on edge and made it hard to concentrate. There was a closed door off to his right. He focused there, panic setting in, trying to determine whether incubi were getting their ends away in that room too. No sign of life.

Payne grabbed Elissa's hand and pulled her towards the door.

Someone appeared in the room behind him.

He whirled to face them, his heart lodged in his throat. Elissa kept her back to them. Relief blasted through him.

The man again.

"I am afraid the master is out and will not return until tomorrow." He preened his dark unruly hair back and smiled. "I have arranged for a room for you. Will you stay the night?"

Payne noticed the way he didn't look at Elissa. His blue and gold eyes remained rooted on him. Payne was still wrestling with the fact that his grandfather didn't just live in this den, he ran it.

Everything in him screamed to refuse and get Elissa the hell away from the constant threat of danger. While he couldn't control her, every incubus here could. He was damned if he was going to let them use their charms on her to get her into bed. She belonged to him.

He couldn't leave though. It would look suspicious.

He forced himself to nod.

The man's smile broadened. "Would you care to join us? There are many willing females here who would feed your every desire. You may enjoy them."

Elissa's nails dug into his hand and rage poured off her. Double interesting. His little witch was jealous.

"No, thank you. I would like to take my mate to our room." Payne made himself smile when all he wanted to do was grimace. Elissa was going to leave marks.

The male eyed her and his lip curled. Payne had the feeling that a mate was not a valued thing in this den of iniquity. Everyone here seemed to be in a race to score the most number of conquests.

The man turned away and Payne pulled on Elissa's hand, making her come with him. They followed the man back through the house, past the orgy that had Payne's blood thundering and his eyes fixing on Elissa to kill the disturbing desire to join in, and up to the first floor. The man led them to the other end of the house, in a very quiet corridor.

Payne couldn't sense anyone in the rooms around them. Relief surged through him, sharp and sweet. Maybe he would retain his sanity and be able to keep a lid on his dark urges to feed after all. He thanked the male with another tight smile and pushed Elissa into the room. She seemed pleased by the green theme that ran through it, from the walls to the covers on the four-poster bed, to the two armchairs in front of the cream marble fireplace. It was definitely a witch thing this time. He had heard they liked nature and nature was green.

He shut the door in the male's face and leaned back against it, tracking her as she moved around the room, snooping at things on the mantelpiece and the wooden table near the armchairs. She disappeared into an adjoining room on his right. The bathroom. Pale green tiles and white porcelain.

Had the incubi bought this place or had they borrowed it from someone? Payne had never thought of that species as a particularly honest one. They had probably taken over the house by force.

He moved to his left and sat on the bed there, waiting for Elissa to emerge. When she did, she looked far happier than she had been in the reception room downstairs. She idly ran her fingers over everything she passed as she crossed the room to him.

He opened his knees and she settled between them, her hands coming to rest on his shoulders. His claimed her waist and he tilted his head back, silently telling her what he wanted from her. She smiled shyly and lowered her mouth towards his, angling her head at the same time. He groaned when she swept her lips across his, soft brushes that ignited his blood and had him hard in his jeans. He needed to feed again. Being around so much sexual energy had him hungry for another taste of his witch.

Elissa pulled away and stroked his cheek. "I think we should rest a while and then we can head out when the house is quiet. Incubi have to sleep at some point and now that I'm near what I'm looking for, I can track it. I'd rather not have to be around them."

Payne could read between the lines. Her fear sang to him through the blood he had taken from her, a connection that wouldn't fade for hours yet. She hadn't liked it when that incubus had tried to control her. He hated it too.

Bewitch

He tipped his head back, enjoying her soft caress and drinking in her beauty, wanting to lure her mouth back to his. "So, we're going to stay here... in this room... with this big bed... just you and me?"

She nodded and ran her index finger along his lower lip, making it tingle. His eyes dropped to his marks on her throat and then met hers again. Her pupils dilated and her lips parted.

"And what if I'm hungry?"

She frowned. "I'm not letting you out of this room so you can fornicate with those bitches."

He raised his eyebrows. "Who said I wanted them?"

Payne pulled her closer and kissed her left breast through her black top. Her nipple beaded beneath the material and he rolled it between his teeth, hungry for his taste of her. She gasped and he drew back.

"You don't want them?" she said, breathless and eyes dark with desire, but touched by a hint of vulnerability.

He shook his head. "I just want you."

"Right answer." She leaned into him and he fell back onto the bed with her on top of him. She rewarded him as she always did, with a soft kiss that made him ache for more and gave him bliss.

Fool around now. Track their items later.

Sounded like a good plan to him. Better than his one, anyway.

He didn't want to meet his grandfather.

He would kill him if he did.

CHAPTER 10

Payne woke to a riot inside of him, a war between two hungers that demanded to be fed. He hadn't caught much sleep. The mansion had him permanently on edge and he couldn't contain his needs. The energy here was intense and overwhelming, far worse than he had ever experienced it at Vampirerotique. It had his incubus side on constant high alert.

He groaned and rolled onto his side under the dark green covers, coming to face Elissa. She stretched beside him, the action causing the sheets to ride down her body, revealing her bare breasts. Tempting. He focused on his body, trying to discern which of his hungers was the most pressing. The incubus in him was restless, roused by the sexual energy flowing through the mansion and hungry for more of his witch.

Elissa settled again, a sigh escaping her soft pink lips. They had fooled around last night but hadn't taken things all the way. It had been enough for him at the time, but now he had one thing on his mind and it drove him to obey. He wanted to be back inside her.

His incubus side purred and prowled around inside him, held at bay by his more dominant vampire nature but not for long. He would indulge it for a change and hopefully he would gain enough satisfaction from what he was going to do with Elissa to last him through the coming hours. The house was still now, the energy in the air less than before. He couldn't hear anyone moving around and most of the heartbeats in the rooms surrounding them were slow and steady, signalling sleep.

It was time they set out in search of his grandfather's room and got what they came here for.

Payne rolled onto his front and eased the covers lower, revealing more of Elissa's beautiful bare curves. He growled low in his throat, his cock hard again and wedged between his body and the firm mattress. She wrinkled her nose in her sleep. He dipped his head and pressed a kiss to her stomach. She sighed.

He smiled.

Payne kissed his way upwards, his eyes on his target. Her breasts. Their dusky pink buds were already pert, calling out for his attention. He swept his lips over her ribs and then along the curve of her right breast. She moaned and the sound cut off.

He flicked a glance at her face.

Elissa stared down her body at him, a sleepy but curious look in her grey eyes. "What are you doing?"

"Waking you up," he whispered against her skin and wrapped his lips around her nipple, eliciting a groan from her.

"Why?" She sounded breathless already and he could smell her desire.

"Because I want you." Payne traced his hand over her stomach and slid it under the green bedclothes, settling it over her curls.

She blushed and bit her lower lip, her eyes hooded and dark with hunger. "Go back to sleep."

She didn't mean that. He slipped his finger into her folds and she moaned, tilting her head back into the rich green pillows. Her chestnut hair spilled around her shoulders in loose waves, dark against her pale creamy skin. She looked like a goddess as she bared herself to him, spreading her thighs so he could delve lower. He eased his hand down and teased her opening, drawing hot moisture from her core and bringing it up to her aroused clitoris. She moaned again, beautifully wanton, the sound stirring fire in his blood and causing his cock to pulse.

Payne pushed the covers down to reveal her long slender legs and moved between them. She gasped as he slid two fingers into her core and lowered his mouth to kiss her. He swirled his tongue around her clitoris, listening to her breathy moans of pleasure and feeding on the energy that flowed from her, basking in how much she enjoyed being with him. She writhed, rocking her hips in time with each thrust of his fingers.

"Payne," she whispered, breathless and low, a plea and a praise at the same time. He groaned into her and licked her from core to aroused nub, savouring the taste of her and wanting more. She lowered her hand to his hair and guided him, silently commanding him even though he was in control now.

The incubus in him purred at the interaction though, especially when she tangled her fingers in his hair and tightly clutched it, forcing him to remain at her clitoris. He lavished it with attention, alternating between flicking it with the tip of his tongue, sensually swirling his tongue around it and laving it.

She moaned and her body tightened around his fingers, drawing him in deeper. He stopped and pulled them out of her, and she groaned and shook her head.

"Why?" she said, hips still rocking, seeking his fingers.

"I want to be inside you when you come."

Her cheeks flushed deep pink and an alluringly innocent expression crossed her beautiful face.

His inner incubus pushed for control over her even though he knew that he couldn't affect her with his charm. The colour on her cheeks darkened and he wondered if she was seeing what he was thinking about, taking her deep and hard, bringing them both to a shattering climax.

"Do you want me inside you?" he whispered and kissed her inner thigh. His incubus charm might not affect her but she wasn't immune to his natural male talents of persuasion.

Elissa nibbled her lower lip and nodded. Payne purred and rose up onto his hands and knees. He moved over her and covered her crotch with his hand. She was so wet beneath his palm, ready for him.

He grasped his cock and dipped his hips.

Elissa shoved against his chest and he stopped to frown down at her.

"Put a condom on." She looked afraid again. He could taste the fear in her blood.

"I only had the one, and it was a miracle I had that... are you not taking anything?" He hovered above her, aching to be inside her again, feeling her body without the barrier this time. She nodded. Problem solved. He lowered himself and she pushed harder against his chest.

He frowned at her again.

Her grey eyes were as wide and bright as full moons. "You can't ejaculate inside me."

Had he just heard her right? He had barely contained himself the last time they had played this game and he wasn't in the mood for it today, not when he was barely controlling his incubus side as it was, and not without a condom as a safety net.

"Playtime is over, Witch. We do this my way now."

She locked her elbows and held him off her. "Seriously. You can't."

Not playing. Rapid heartbeat. Scent of fear in her blood. She wasn't joking at all.

Payne sat back and fixed her with a black look. "Why don't you want my seed within you?"

She hesitated. His anger spiked and he stepped off the bed, distancing himself physically because he was having difficulty doing it emotionally. His head swam with reasons, taunts that drove him to the brink and had him feeling like a complete fool.

"Is it because I'm a vampire? I know witches don't like vampires but you seemed to like riding my cock before."

She sat up, drawing the covers over her, and shook her head. Her silvery eyes drifted down to his chest. No, not his chest. His biceps and the markings that snaked over them.

He growled at her, anger combining with the hurt that clawed his heart to pieces and becoming rage. He folded his arms across his chest and bared his fangs at her.

"I see. I get it. You don't want to risk bearing the offspring of an abomination." He turned his back on her and stared at the dark grate of the fireplace, struggling against the crushing weight of the pain in his chest. "I should have known. You've got what you wanted... used me to get you here... and now you want nothing to do with me."

A breeze shifted behind him, across his backside, and Elissa grabbed his arm. He refused to heed her command when she tugged on it and remained facing away from her. She pulled harder and Payne turned on her, snapping his arm out of her grip and smacking her hand away when she tried to touch him again.

She flinched and cried out, the sound startling in the quiet room, and clutched her left wrist to her chest. Tears swam in her eyes and he could feel the pain beating in her heart, rushing through her blood. He had heard the bone crack.

He stopped himself from taking a step towards her and took a step back instead. "That was your fault."

She didn't deny it. She simply held her wrist and stared at him in silence. His guilt couldn't erase his rage and his pain. It did nothing to dampen it and he only felt worse as he looked at her. He turned away again, unable to bear the sight of her now that he knew the truth.

"Payne?" she softly whispered his name and it stirred heat within him that he pretended not to feel.

He looked over his shoulder at her. Her silver eyes were beautiful, glittering with diamond dust as she used her magic to heal her broken wrist.

"It was my fault." She looked down at her arm and then back up into his eyes. "And it isn't about offspring or you being an incubus."

He roared. "I'm a vampire."

She shrank back, her fear flooding the room, and nodded even though he could see in her eyes that she wanted to mention that he wasn't wholly vampire. He hated her for it but it didn't stop him from wanting her. She fascinated him and made him weak, stripped his strength away and left him needing her, willing to do anything for another taste or touch.

Desperate to do anything to win her heart.

Impossible.

She had proven that barely a few minutes ago. His little witch wasn't his after all. She had merely played him for a fool to make him do exactly as she had wanted. She had manipulated him.

He growled and glared at her, not hiding any of his anger or hurt. He wanted her to see what she had done. He needed her to know just how much she had hurt him and that things would never be the same between them.

"Witches are not supposed to mate with demons, and dark fae species like incubi are considered demons by my kind and others," she whispered, as though afraid to voice it any louder in case it drew a violent reaction from him.

He kept his head and spoke calmly even though he wanted to grab her and scream it down her ear so she would finally get the message. "I'm not a demon. I'm a vampire."

She didn't nod this time. His hatred of her grew as she stared straight into his eyes in that way that always made him feel as though she was tearing his mask away to reveal the ugly truth beneath. He turned his back on her again.

"Don't leave." She moved behind him but stopped short of grabbing him. She was learning after all.

He wasn't sure how he would react if she touched him again. His incubus and vampire sides were both angry and hurt, both out for blood and violence because neither understood why their mate had betrayed them. He didn't understand. She was supposed to be his. He had foolishly begun to believe that the wonderful, incredible time they had spent together would blossom into something he had only ever dreamed would happen to him. He had wanted a mate. He almost laughed at himself.

He had spent so long denying his nature and his needs, shutting down his emotions and keeping his distance to protect himself, that he hadn't realised that he wanted that from Elissa. He needed her to be his salvation. He had begun to hope that she would be the good that would balance out the bad in his life, the reward at the end of so much pain.

"I didn't mean to upset you. It's just... I have my reasons." Her voice was soft, edged with warmth and concern that only hurt him all the more because he wasn't sure how to react around or how to feel about her now.

"Other than using me to come here?" He wouldn't let that one go. She had been gunning for him from the moment they had met. She had wanted to get into his pants and she had succeeded in doing what his last lover had failed to do. She had enslaved him, but rather than using his name to do it, she had used her body as the lure and his own heart as the shackles.

He pressed his hand to his chest and cursed himself for being idiotic enough to trust anyone again, let alone a witch.

"Please, Payne. Let me explain," she said and he did her an honour she didn't deserve.

He turned to face her because he needed to see in her eyes that she believed whatever poison was about to come out of her pretty mouth. She looked lost as she stood before him, body bare, vulnerable. He probably looked the same. Weak and pathetic. Easily broken.

"Explain away." He grabbed his boxer shorts from the floor and slipped his legs into them, tugged them up, and let the elastic snap against his waist.

Elissa didn't dress.

She twisted her hands in front of her stomach, her gaze on the floor, and then frowned and looked up into his eyes. "You came to the town to find another witch."

He nodded. "You said you were covering for her. Verity, wasn't it?"

Tears rose into her eyes again and she scrubbed them away with the heel of her hand and nodded. "Verity... was my older sister."

"Something tells me you lied." He hated that but the hurt swimming in her eyes said that she had a good reason, and now he knew why she had looked ready to cry that day in her home. "She's dead?"

Elissa swallowed hard and nodded again.

"Did my grandfather kill her?"

A shake this time.

She moved to the bed on legs that shook so much he was surprised she reached it without collapsing and sat down, her hands between her knees. He had never seen her looking so lost and he wanted to go to her. It was hard to hold himself back but he had to. Until he knew this hadn't all been a twisted game to her, he needed to maintain his distance. It wouldn't stop the pain that ebbed and flowed through him, growing weaker and stronger by turns, but it would stop her from completely destroying his soul if he discovered that he was right about her and she had used him.

"When a witch takes demon seed into her body, it taints her powers... the connection to her coven is also tainted and she weakens dramatically. Witches draw on their coven to boost their natural abilities. The more there are in a coven, the stronger each witch becomes. If a witch..." She drew her legs up onto the bed and wrapped her arms around them, looking small and uncertain as she eyed him. Didn't she want to tell him? He moved a step closer, aching to reassure her that he wanted to know about her so he could understand everything. "Verity had a fling with a demon. She took precautions but it didn't stop her connection from becoming tainted. The coven exercised their right to deal with her."

"They killed her?" It sounded barbaric to Payne and now he could see why Elissa was so afraid. She didn't want to suffer the same horrific fate as her sister.

"She knew they were coming... had found her. She asked me to take care of something for her and I swore that I would. I tried so hard to keep it hidden because I knew how precious it had been to Verity."

"My grandfather took it from you though." What had she sworn to conceal? Whatever it was, it was important to Elissa. He could see it in her eyes and now he understood why she had fought so hard to come with him to this place. She had to fulfil her promise to her dead sister and protect this item.

"And I want it back." She glanced into his eyes and then off to his right, at the unlit fire. "I didn't use you, Payne... and I do want you... I'm crazily attracted to you even when I know how dangerous that is."

"Maybe you just want me because I'm dangerous." It was a sound theory but Elissa's frown told him that it wasn't the case.

"I think it has more to do with your ridiculously good looks and that body." She waved a hand down the length of him and actually smiled.

Payne's heart missed a beat. He was glad she had found her smile again and that the sombreness in her eyes had lifted. The sight of it eased the ache in his chest and he couldn't hold on to his anger. It slipped from his grasp and he looked her over, seeing the hint of vulnerability that still edged her eyes. She looked small as she sat alone, waiting for him to react or perhaps retaliate. He sighed and decided to be the better man and let it go. He already had enough reasons to feel angry. He didn't need to add Elissa to the list, not when she was the one good thing in his dark world.

"I said you just wanted to get into my pants." He grinned, gunning for charming again, and crossed the room to her. She patted the bed beside her, a peace offering that he gladly accepted. He sat down and took hold of her left arm, gently inspecting her wrist. The bone felt whole again, no sign of a break. "I'm sorry about that."

She shrugged. "I should have explained myself better... I didn't mean to make you feel that way."

Elissa leaned her head against his shoulder and he slipped his fingers between hers, holding her hand. He stared down at them. Where the hell did he go from here? Elissa tied him in knots and had him on the edge all the time, looking for hidden meanings in everything she said. Did he want her to be out to use him or only in this to hurt him in some way? Why couldn't he trust her?

"Payne?" she whispered, her soft voice warming his heart and easing the pain away. She looked up at him and then pressed her lips to his bare shoulder, lingering there.

"Elissa?" he said when he realised that she wouldn't continue without him prompting her. She felt tense, her anxiety flowing over him, carried by her scent. What had she wanted to ask but was now too afraid to voice?

Payne gently squeezed her hand and she looked up at him again. He kept his expression soft and open, hoping it would soothe her and help her find her voice. She could ask whatever she wanted and he would answer her this time because he no longer wanted any barriers between them. He wanted to know her, wanted to break through everything that had happened in the past few minutes and find solid ground with her again.

"Why do you feel you deserve pain?" she breathed the words against his skin, her lips brushing him at the same time, stirring heat and desire in his veins.

His guard was down and he realised for the first time in his life that he ached to tell someone and share the burden. Would she turn on him if she knew? He thought that she might. She would want nothing to do with him.

But he needed to tell her.

CHAPTER 11

Payne let go of her hand and Elissa thought he would refuse to answer her. She could almost feel him distancing himself as he moved to lie on the bed, slung his left arm behind his head on the pillows and laid his right across his bare stomach. Was he going to give her the silent treatment again? He didn't look at her. His dark grey eyes fixed on the green canopy of the four-poster bed, the flecks of blue and gold in them bright against their stony backdrop. There was a touch of red edging his irises though. What was he thinking to make them change, veering towards their vampire state?

He drew in a deep breath and sighed it out.

"I was born to an elite bloodline and my parents were very loving towards me."

Elissa's eyes widened. He was going to tell her. He was actually going to answer the one question that always seemed to set him on edge. Was it because she had talked about her family with him? It had hurt her to speak about her sister, even when she had kept most of the details about her hidden from Payne still. The colours of his fae markings shifted, the change beginning along the underside of his arms and working up the lines of symbols towards his shoulders. They gradually darkened to shades of ash and blood. He was angry but the distant look in his eyes said that it wasn't directed at her.

Purple and blue bloomed along his markings, swirling and mixing with the black and the red. Hurt. How did he feel about those markings? Did he hate that they gave everything away about his feelings? She had once thought that he could control them to a degree, masking his feelings.

Maybe he couldn't, or he wasn't as good at it as she had thought, because she could see all of his feelings in his markings.

Or maybe she was reading too far into things, and he was letting her see his feelings. If that was the case, then it touched her that he was letting his guard down.

"I should probably correct that... my parents were loving towards me at first." He closed his eyes and exhaled again, causing his torso to shift in a beautiful wave that lured her eyes to it. She forced them back to his face, refusing to stare at him while he was opening his heart to her. He tilted his head towards her and opened his eyes. "We were a close family and my father adored my mother. He had turned her long before they decided to have a child and I loved her as deeply as my father, adoring her too."

The warmth in his eyes and the slight tilt of his sensual lips conveyed how much he had loved his mother. She hadn't failed to notice that he was talking past tense. Something had happened to Payne's happy family.

"I grew up in a mansion with other families but my father was the head of the bloodline. He indulged my every whim, spoiling me and my mother." His eyelids dropped again, shuttering his beautiful eyes, but she hadn't missed the darkness that had entered them just a second before he had closed them, shutting her out. "I was on the verge of puberty when my fae markings appeared."

"You weren't born with them?" Her heart missed a beat and lodged in her throat, trembling there. Verity had been wrong. Elissa had hoped that her sister had been right and that Luca only had witch in his genes. She had prayed to the earth and the sky that Luca had inherited none of his father's genes. Now she knew without a doubt that those prayers had gone unanswered. Luca would develop his markings when he matured.

Payne shook his head. "I tried to hide them. I was scared and I didn't know what they meant. I didn't understand them and why I had them. I tried to make them go away. I was scrubbing myself raw in the bath one day when a servant entered and saw them. She told my father."

"What happened?" Elissa lay next to him on the bed and risked placing her hand over his right one where it rested on his stomach. He didn't pull away. He spread his fingers and let her slip hers between them, her palm pressing against the back of his hand.

"I had never seen my father so angry. He was enraged and distraught, his anger flowing freely, disturbing the whole house. He dragged me from the bath and held me by the back of my neck. He marched me through the house in search of my mother." Payne looked into Elissa's eyes and she squeezed his hand, wishing she could do more, could take away his hurt and shame. "He found my mother in the entrance hall, just returned from riding. The whole house had gathered to stare. She was horrified that I was nude before everyone, my skin red raw. She argued with my father."

"She thought he had hurt you." What affectionate mother wouldn't think such a thing on seeing her son being treated in such a disgusting way?

Payne nodded. "It was only when my father accused her of sleeping with another male and shouted that I wasn't his that she truly looked at me. She saw the marks on my skin... I could sense her confusion... or perhaps it was my own."

Elissa shuffled closer to him and kept quiet this time. The red edging his eyes, slowly eating away all the other colours, warned that he wouldn't want her sympathy if she offered it. He wanted her to listen without interrupting, and she would. She would let him do this at his own pace because he clearly needed to tell her. She only hoped it was cathartic for him.

He shifted his gaze back to the canopy. The blue and gold in his eyes swirled, and he gained a distant, unfocused expression. His markings darkened again to obsidian and crimson.

"Mother swore to my father that she hadn't betrayed him and she loved him with all of her heart. I can remember her voice and her pain, her fear. I remember it all as if it were yesterday. It haunts me. She told my father that she didn't know why I bore my markings or what they meant." He sighed and the hurt surfaced on those markings again, tinting them purple and blue in places and increasing the black. "Father wouldn't listen to her. The whole family stared down at me and I was afraid they would turn on me and ask me what I was. I didn't know. I was confused and scared, and unsure of myself. I felt alien... wrong... disgusting. An abomination. I ached for my father and mother to look down at me too and tell me that nothing had changed and they loved me still, and that together we would come to understand what the weird symbols meant and why I had them."

He closed his eyes and a tear slipped down from the corner of his lashes. He shifted his left arm out from behind his head and threw it across his eyes, hiding them from her.

Elissa tightened her grip on his hand, her heart aching for him. Her anger rose too.

Payne had done nothing wrong and his parents must have felt his fear and confusion, but they had done nothing to reassure him. His father had paraded him in front of the family, shaming him and making him feel as though he was an outsider, an object to stare at with disgust. He had degraded his own son, the boy he had claimed to love.

"When my father looked at me at last, there had been only coldness in his eyes. I turned to my mother but she refused to look at me, even when I fell on my knees and begged her."

Mother earth, what cruelty they had inflicted upon him, their boy who had looked up to them and loved them with all of his heart. He had only wanted their love in return, just as they had given it to him unconditionally before his markings had surfaced. Payne's fingers squeezed hers, hurting her. She didn't let her pain show. He needed to hold on to her and she wouldn't deny him anything that would comfort him. He could break her fingers and she still wouldn't let go of his hand. She wouldn't let him suffer alone. Not as his parents had.

"My father ordered that I be taken out of his sight. Someone took me away. I don't remember who. I only remember the shame that burned in me and the way everyone whispered as I passed, staring at me and my cursed markings."

He lifted his arm and looked at her. He looked so lost and broken that she wanted to touch his cheek, needed him to know that she was here with him and that she felt for him. She managed to hold her tongue and keep still, knowing that he needed to keep going now that he had started.

"My mother tried to convince my father that she hadn't cheated on him with another male. I heard them arguing all the time over the coming weeks. They would fall silent whenever they saw me, and would turn away, neither of them willing to listen to me. In the end, they made me remain in my quarters. I lost everything. My family turned their backs on me one by one, shunning me. My father probably ordered it."

His gaze roamed back to the canopy above them.

Elissa's heart went out to him. She couldn't imagine how he must have felt. Just a boy, scared and uncertain, unsure of what he was and what his markings meant, mistreated by those he loved and relied upon. He had gone from being the centre of his parents' world to an object of hate and disgust. He had suffered so much, had been treated so poorly, dejected and disgraced, left to struggle with the changes happening in him alone when someone should have been there to hold him and guide him, to love him.

"My father refused to believe my mother because she couldn't offer solid proof that she hadn't cheated on him. They argued about me for months, growing more and more distant from each other, and from me. My father moved into the other wing of the mansion, as far from my mother as he could get. He refused to speak to her or me."

He tensed and stared in silence at the canopy, his eyes blank, as though he was miles away from her. What pain was he reliving now? Tears slipped down his temple into his sandy hair and Elissa couldn't stop herself anymore. She moved closer to him, rolling so her chest pressed against the side of his torso, and stroked his hair with her left hand while retaining her grip on his right.

His eyes dropped to her and he looked more lost and broken than she had ever seen him.

His voice cracked as he spoke. "My final memory of my mother is of her embracing the sun."

He swallowed hard and didn't look as though he could continue. Struggle shone in his eyes and flickered across his face, twisting his handsome visage into a pained grimace. She stroked his hair, gently running her fingers over the tousled sandy spikes, trying to give him some peace in the midst of so much suffering. She wished she had never asked him why he had chosen to call himself Payne or why he felt he deserved to suffer now. She had never meant to inflict this hurt upon him.

It pained her to see her strong, powerful male so hurt and weak, suffering and vulnerable, wrestling with his past and his feelings. It was little wonder he despised his incubus side and couldn't accept it, and sought pain as a remedy to his desires. He had probably never stopped hurting in the centuries that had likely passed since he had been shunned as a boy.

He carried his pain with him, an eternal torment, a poison that bred doubt in his mind, making him believe that no one could feel anything positive towards him. His family had instilled in him a belief that no one could ever love him as he was because he was an abomination, something that should be detested and scorned, not cherished and adored.

She could see that now, and she hated them for it. She wanted to seek out his family and punish them all for the pain that they had inflicted upon an innocent, warping his perspective of the world and causing him to despise himself and his mixed blood.

He sucked in a sharp breath. "I hadn't been able to sleep and had felt her pause outside my room before moving on down the hallway. I followed her down to the entrance hall and found her standing near the double doors. She looked at me with so much pain in her eyes, so much misery, and then threw open the doors to the garden and let the sunlight stream over her." His voice hitched and cracked again, and he ground his teeth, tears streaming from the corners of his eyes and his eyebrows knitting tightly. "I tried to stop her but I failed. I was too young. My hands caught fire. I wanted to die in her place... if I couldn't have that... then I wanted to die with her."

Tears filled Elissa's eyes and she sniffed them back, her heart breaking for him. He had clearly adored his mother as much as he had said, and felt responsible for her decision to commit suicide. She stroked his cheek, his cool skin damp with tears beneath her fingers. He had suffered so much because of his mixed genes. She had never anticipated, had never dreamed, that he had been through so much. It was little wonder that he hated his incubus side now and wanted nothing to do with it. She couldn't blame him for it either. It had stripped away all that he loved and had cherished, and something told Elissa that his suffering hadn't ended at his mother's death.

"The next thing I remember is waking in a dark room, in my parents' bed. I thought perhaps someone had saved my mother and I was resting with her. When my vision cleared, I saw my father lying beside me, his arms swathed in bloodstained bandages." He closed his eyes again and pinched the bridge of his nose. She gave him a moment to gather himself and brushed her fingers over his hair, letting him know that she was still there for him. "I was covered in bandages too. Every inch of me... all of them stained crimson. I wanted to cry but I stifled my pain and loss. When my father stirred, I expected him to make me leave. Instead, he drew me to him and told me that he had never meant for this to happen. I hated him."

Understandable. His father had driven his mother to kill herself.

"I hated my father but I blamed myself for her death. I spent years looking for information on fae and searching for a way to clear my mother's name. When I discovered that my mother's bloodline had an incubus in it, her father, and that all of the children he had sired with her mother had been female and therefore not incubi, but a carrier of those genes, I grew enraged at my father." Payne slipped his hand free of hers and wiped his eyes, clearing away his tears. Elissa looked at Payne's markings nearest his wrist. She didn't recognise the symbols there, at the top of his lineage. His mother's name written in the fae tongue? "My mother hadn't known that she had incubus blood in her. I challenged my father and my father banished me, but not before I fought him. My father swore he never wanted to see me again."

"What happened?"

"I left and lived in the world alone. I grew up without my family, watching them from a distance. When I had matured and was stronger, I went back to see my family. I needed to know if I could return." The darkness in his tone said that they had denied him and her heart ached again, a deep throbbing that made her want to wrap her arms around him and hold him, and whisper that his family should have taken him back. He had only wanted to be with those he loved, even though they had hurt him. "I argued with my father. He blamed me for my mother's death, accused me of ripping his heart out and destroying him. I countered him, accusing him of being the one who had torn out my heart and destroyed me, humiliated and shattered me. He struck me repeatedly, blaming me all the while, telling me I had killed my mother. I will never forget that night."

Payne rubbed his right arm and Elissa stared down at it, at the scars that littered his skin. What had his father done to him? It was bad enough that Payne had to live with the scars on his heart and his soul, haunted by his memories, but his father had done something to place scars on his body too, so he could never forget.

"I lost my head. I fought back and shoved him. He fell near the fire, picked up one of the irons and flew at me. I tried to defend myself. He broke my arm with the iron and didn't stop. He kept hitting me, shattering the bone, breaking through my skin. After the seventh strike, the pain overwhelmed me. I had no control over myself. I attacked and got the poker from my father. The next thing I recall is my father staring at me, blood pouring from his lips, scarcely breathing. I looked down and I saw what I had done." Payne closed his eyes and frowned, his whole body tensing. Elissa stroked his arm, running her fingers up and down, needing to do something for him. "I had skewered my father with the poker. I had driven it under his breastbone and straight through his heart... I had gone to the house to ask my father to take me back and love me again, and I had ended up killing him. I was no better than my father had accused me of being."

He turned his head and opened his eyes, looking straight into hers.

"I am a monster."

She shook her head, unwilling to believe that because it wasn't true. His father had made him feel as though he was wrong in some way, an abomination and a monster. He had driven his son to murder, wounding him so badly that his vampire instincts had seized control and forced him to defend himself, driven by a dark need to survive. It wasn't his fault at all. All of the blame rested at his father's feet.

"You asked why I called myself Payne. I called myself Payne so I would always remember what I had been through, a constant reminder of how easy it was to make someone suffer, and that love could kill as easily as a blade."

Elissa felt so sorry for him. He stared at her, grey eyes edged with red but dull and full of unshed tears. Tension flowed from him in waves and lines bracketed his dusky lips. She knew that he was waiting for her to judge him and that there was some part of him that wanted her to hate him, needed it, because he felt he deserved it. He wanted her to tell him that she believed he was an abomination now, a disgusting creature that didn't deserve her affection.

A monster.

Elissa laid her palm on his cheek. "You're not a monster. You only wanted your father to love you. You only wanted your family again. You did nothing wrong. They were the ones in the wrong. They all turned on you because you were different and that wasn't your fault. They should have accepted you for what you were, not rejected you because of it. They should have loved you, Payne."

He looked away from her, causing her hand to slip from his face. "No one can love a monster."

Elissa wasn't sure what else she could say to make him believe her. His parents had turned on him for something that was beyond his control and not his fault. His mate had tried to force him to change and had then betrayed him by using his trust against him, trying to enslave him to her will by using his real name. Now, Elissa had made him embrace his incubus side and had brought him to the place where his grandfather lived, and gods only knew what he was going to do when he saw the man. She had the terrible feeling that he would kill him for what he had done to his family.

"Say something." His voice was hoarse and his grey eyes both challenged and begged her at the same time.

Elissa still wasn't sure what to say, so she craned her neck and kissed him. He was quick to respond, his lips dancing with hers, a desperate and hungry edge to his movements. He needed this more than he needed words. She would show him that he was wrong.

Payne slid his arm around her and pulled her on top of him. He held her there, his hands grasping her backside, as he kissed her. She allowed him to master her, his aggressive kisses sending a hot rush through her and making her head spin until she felt dizzy, drunk on his passion and his desire for her.

She didn't think he was a monster.

His pained confession had only awoken dangerous feelings in her, ones that ran deeper than compassion. He had reached out and grabbed her heart, and now she wasn't sure what to do, but there was one thing she knew.

She was falling for him, and it was already too late to save herself.

CHAPTER 12

Payne wasn't sure how to act around Elissa. He strolled along the bare pale blue corridor, his boots heavy on the wooden floor, heading away from their room with her trailing along beside him. She hadn't said much since he had bared all and let her see beyond the barrier, but the way she looked at him each time he chanced a glance at her reassured him that she honestly believed he wasn't a monster.

He looked at her out of the corner of his eye and she smiled at him, silvery eyes warm with what might have been affection. He wanted to believe that it was. He needed to hold on to hope that Elissa might become the one great thing in his life, the reward he wanted her to be, not another person that would end up cutting him to the bone and leaving him alone in this world.

Her fingers stroked his left palm and he didn't stop her. He let her slide her hand into his and then shifted his, linking their fingers to heighten the connection between them. He liked doing this with her. He had held hands with women before, but not this way, with fingers locked together.

He had always tried to keep a distance, even from the woman he had thought was his true mate.

He could see that now that he was with Elissa. With her, he wanted to be as close as he could get, joined in ways that felt permanent and secure. He had slept with her locked tightly in his embrace, held flush against him, constantly aware of her body pressing into his, all softness and warmth, her feminine scent filling his lungs and her steady heartbeat sounding in his ears, a rhythm that had soothed him and kept the nightmares at bay.

He had never been into the poetic or romantic shit, but he kept wondering whether the needs he felt around her, the constant pressing urge to touch her in some way and be linked to her, was because she was his true mate.

His little witch.

Both sides of him purred in approval.

Payne tugged his hand behind his back, forcing her to follow her arm and press against his side. He turned into her, wrapped his free arm around her waist, and dragged her closer. He lowered his mouth and claimed her lips, stealing her moist sweet breath with his kiss. She moaned and rather than pushing him away and chastising him for slowing them down, pulled him closer and ran her hand around the nape of his neck.

The feel of her fingers ploughing through his hair sent a shiver dancing over his nerve endings and lit up his hunger, igniting his need for her. He walked with her, his mouth dominating hers, tongues tangling and teasing, and pressed her into the wall. She moaned, the sound sweet in his ears, and clawed his scalp, ripping a groan from his throat.

"Witch," he growled into her mouth and kissed her harder, claiming more of her, unable to control himself now that she had turned wicked. A hot bolt of lust struck him right to his soul and he shoved her harder against the wall. Elissa wriggled against him. Payne grabbed her bottom and lifted her. She wrapped her legs around his waist and he rolled his eyes, groaning again as they locked around his backside.

He rocked into her, already hard and aching in his jeans. She moaned breathily against his lips, the soft puff of air driving him out of control.

Payne snarled and kissed her again.

She tensed.

They weren't alone.

Payne lifted his head and slowly turned it to face the intruder. An incubus stood in the open doorway of one of the rooms down the hall to his right, naked as the day he had been born, his hand on his cock, slowly stroking it. The sure look in his blue and gold eyes, the way he smiled right at Elissa, and the fact that she reacted, pushed Payne over the edge.

He dropped Elissa, teleported to the man, grabbed him by the throat and slammed him hard into the doorframe, knocking the breath from him.

Payne stepped into him and roared in his face, baring his fangs and tightening his grip on the man's throat at the same time, digging his claws in to draw blood. The incubus choked and grimaced, and grappled with Payne's arm, trying to prise it away from him. Payne snarled again, getting in the man's face, ensuring the dark haired male knew he was treading on thin ice and that he wouldn't get a warning next time he turned on the charm with Elissa.

"Payne," Elissa whispered and he refused to heed her command. He couldn't let this male think that a female ruled him and could easily bring him to heel.

Payne tightened his grip, throttling the male who had challenged him. He growled, flashing fangs again, his eyes red and sharp, his vampire side fully in control. "Mine. Understand?"

The male frantically nodded.

Payne released him and then landed a hard right hook on his jaw for good measure, sending him crashing onto the wooden floor. It took all of his willpower to force himself to step away and not level a hard kick at his stomach while he was down.

He turned to face Elissa.

She stood with her back pressed against the wall. There was a nervous edge to her beautiful face and her heartbeat, but the scent of desire continued to roll off her and her enlarged pupils said that his display of aggression, the things he had said, and his possessive behaviour had aroused her.

He growled back at the man and then stalked towards her. He was barely within a metre of her when she threw herself into his arms, hers instantly looping around his neck and dragging him down to her. She kissed him hard, dominating him this time, and he wanted to take her back to their room and forget their treasure hunt.

He dragged her against him, bending her to his will, taking control of the kiss and telling her without words that he had meant what he had said. She was his now, and he would challenge any male who tried to change that.

Sounds came from below them and his focus shifted there, his vampire hearing picking up fragments of a conversation between two males. One mentioned a visitor, his voice familiar. The man who had escorted them to the room. His grandfather's assistant. Had his grandfather returned?

Payne drew away from Elissa and focused his senses on the world outside. It smelled faintly of sunshine, but in a lingering way that signalled it was close to sunset. Daylight had come and gone. They had failed to take advantage of the time they'd had to search the mansion for his grandfather's rooms, too lost in each other to notice the hours slipping past.

The deep unfamiliar male voice sounded mildly surprised as he responded and then mentioned something about resting before they met. Payne pulled in a slow breath, using it to steady himself and the nerves that were beginning to grow out of control inside him. His grandfather. His heart thumped against his chest, hard and fast, the tempo increasing as he thought about how a meeting between them might play out. He would do his best to control his urge to make his grandfather pay for everything his mother had suffered, and all he had been through too, not because he didn't want to kill the man, but because he had to keep Elissa safe. If he attacked the male who ran this den, he would cause the other incubi to retaliate. He would place Elissa in danger.

"What is it?" Elissa whispered, her eyes enormous and fixed on him.

"He's here."

She tensed in his arms and stared along the hall, the wavy fall of her chestnut hair masking her face and her heartbeat sounding rapidly in his head. Her fear blasted off her in strong waves, crashing over him and drawing his vampire side to the fore again. He was hungry. Payne's gaze dropped to the creamy curves of her breasts in her black halter-top. His heart accelerated.

She caught him staring and her frown was chastisement enough. He apologised with a wicked smile, and a touch of pink coloured her cheeks. He still loved it whenever he made her blush like an innocent. She couldn't know what it did to him, how it tugged at not only his protective instincts but his constant hunger for her, otherwise she wouldn't blush so easily. She would try to control it from fear of him biting her again.

Lord above, he wanted to bite her again.

His fangs lengthened and his cock hardened painfully in his jeans. Saliva pooled in his mouth and his mind dived back to the one time he had taken her blood, filling his senses with the taste of her essence. Hunger gnawed at his gut.

"We're clearly not going to get anywhere looking for his room anyway." She raised an eyebrow at him and pointedly dropped her gaze to his crotch and the bulge there. "You can't take a step in his place without looking like you're concealing a dangerous weapon in your jeans."

If what she had said was true, and his seed was enough to have her coven out to execute her, then he wasn't looking as though he was concealing a dangerous weapon. He was concealing one. The last thing he wanted to do was get her in trouble with her coven, or put her in the firing line, but he wasn't sure how much longer he could deny his need for her.

He shoved his fingers through the dirty blond spikes of his hair and gripped them hard, trying to figure out what to do. He needed to meet his grandfather and get his scent. Elissa could remain in the room, safe from harm, and sleep while he dealt with their dual problem. If he was lucky, the bastard would want to meet him in his quarters rather than a reception room and Payne wouldn't have to sniff around the house to find their location.

He grabbed Elissa's hand and headed back to their room. She entered first and he paused to watch her as she crossed the room to the fire and used her magic to start it. The flames lit her face, warming her pale skin and turning her eyes golden. She was beautiful, arresting. He had thought it the first time he had laid eyes on her and every time since. Whenever he took a moment to just look at her, it struck him anew, filling him with a sensation of need and awareness like he had never felt before. He could watch her for hours, days, years, and he would never grow tired of just looking at her. Her expression changed so rapidly, never concealing her emotions, always allowing them to show.

Did she do this with everyone or was she allowing him to see more of her than she showed to others? He could imagine that she had been like this with her sister, open and unguarded, never hiding anything.

Elissa paused halfway through placing another log onto the fire and turned her head towards him, her eyes slowly lifting to meet his. Golden light played across her skin, flickering and dancing in her soft brown hair. She looked like an angel, kneeling on the rug before him, wearing a halo of pure gold.

"Elissa," he breathed and she rose to her feet, turning fully towards him. He wasn't sure what he had wanted to say to her. It slipped from his grasp and he ended up staring at her in silence, drinking in the way she looked at him, not as though he was a monster, but as though he was a man.

A man who she wanted.

A man who she might grow to love.

"You should get some rest." His voice sounded distant even to his ears. It wasn't what he had wanted to say to her. He had meant to ask her to come to him and let him kiss her again, let him touch her and ruin her, because he needed her more than air or a heartbeat, or anything in this world.

She took a step towards the bed and then paused again. "Will you come too?"

He shook his head. She would be too tempting and he didn't want to ruin her, not really. She would never forgive him if he did.

He would never forgive himself.

She shifted course and approached him rather than the bed. He held his hands up and backed off a step. The house was coming alive again, the energy that constantly swirled around him increasing in strength and setting his incubus side on edge. Coupled with his intense craving to taste her blood again, he was only a danger to her right now.

"What's wrong?" she whispered, a frown marring her beauty, turning her eyes dark.

"If you come near me... I won't be able to stop myself. You have to understand... I'm on the edge, Elissa. Both sides of me are hungry for you... I don't want to place you in danger."

She hesitated and he couldn't blame her. The gold and blue were probably swirling in his eyes by now, red and pink flushing his markings and announcing his aroused state to her as well as his deep hunger.

Elissa held his gaze and took another step towards him.

"What are you doing?" He backed off another step and she smiled, a sensual one that stole his breath and beat at his defences and control.

She didn't stop. She kept advancing and he kept retreating, but he was shit out of luck. His back hit the closed door. He considered teleporting but he wasn't fast enough. Before he could think of a location to leap to, she had closed the distance between them and had pressed her hot palms against his chest, searing him through his dark grey shirt and branding his very bones with her name.

His hunger spiked, the twin urges swirling together and combining, turning him dangerous. He had only ever experienced such a need once in his lifetime, and he hadn't been able to control himself then. He had come close to killing the woman he had once loved.

He wouldn't be able to live with himself if he hurt Elissa like that.

He cared too much about her.

He caught both of her cheeks in his palms and forced her to look up at him. "I don't want to hurt you."

His hands shook almost as much as his voice had. Her smile stole his heart and the way she lifted her hands and covered his, holding them against her face, had him quaking with need.

"You won't. I want to do this, Payne." She drew his right hand away from her face and kissed his palm, and then trailed her lips to his wrist. She followed the line of his fae markings, kissing them, stirring his hunger to new heights.

"But... I might not be able to hold off."

She paused then and he felt her shaking, sensed her fear. His vampire side fed on it, hungry to taste more, to scare her until she visibly trembled. He tamped it down. Elissa was his mate.

Payne froze as the certainty of those words struck him.

Where had his doubt gone?

He looked down into her eyes and felt sure that he was right and that Elissa did belong to him now, and forever. She had worked her way into his heart and he had told her all of his dark secrets. He had confessed everything and let her see a side of him that he had hidden from everyone, even his last love. He had kept his distance from them all, had lived alone in this world surrounded by people, but he hadn't been able to keep Elissa at arm's length. He had only been able to draw her into his embrace and felt the need to hold her close to him and never let her go.

"I can do a spell," she said and she sounded so sure that Payne could no longer deny his twin hungers.

He swooped on her mouth and kissed her, determined to possess all of her.

After this time, things would never be the same between them again.

After this time, Elissa would belong to him.

She would be his mate.

CHAPTER 13

Elissa knew something was off with Payne. Different. She could sense it within him, a hunger and need she hadn't noticed before. He had acted possessively with that other male and had claimed she belonged to him. Did he truly believe that? She knew about vampires and that many claimed mates. She didn't know how they did it, or how an incubus knew or claimed their mate either. Did Payne truly believe that she was his mate?

What if she was?

Did she want to bind herself to Payne?

He scooped her up into his arms and carried her to the bed. She thought he would toss her onto it but he gently laid her down, almost reverently, and leaned over to kiss her. She melted into the dark green covers, giving herself over to his kiss and the passion it stirred in her veins. His tongue stroked the seam of her lips and she opened for him, allowing him to enter her mouth and tangle his tongue with hers, flooding her with his taste. Hunger sparked within her, stronger than before, desire that threatened to control her actions. She tried to focus, knowing that if she didn't cast her spell soon she would be too far gone, too hungry to have Payne inside her, his long cock filling her up, to care about the consequences.

Payne kissed along her jaw and she mourned the loss of his mouth on hers, ached for him to return. He reached her throat and moved over her, positioning one knee between her thighs, his hands pressing into the mattress on either side of her ribs.

"My spell will probably stop you from coming until I lift it... you're sure you're okay with that?" It wasn't the most romantic or erotic conversation to have while a gorgeous man was sucking on her pulse point and driving her wild with need, but it was necessary, and she had always been focused on doing things that were necessary. Verity had joked that she would never live life because she spent too much time following orders and refusing to take risks.

Her sister would be proud of her.

Here she was, on the verge of allowing a demon inside her without any form of protection other than a spell.

It was hard to concentrate with Payne licking and nipping at her throat, sending shivers coursing over her arms and down her spine.

He growled against her skin and she tried again.

"You're okay with this?"

He pulled back this time, the colours in his eyes already brightening, his pupils wide with desire.

He nodded.

Why did she have the feeling he would have agreed to anything she had said? Was he even listening to her? If she had said the moon really was made of cheese, would he have nodded?

"You know, the moon is made of cheese?" She shrugged when he frowned at her. "I was just testing."

"I'm fine with this," he husked, desire dripping from his deep voice, and she shivered again, a hot rush of need racing through her blood.

"Mother earth, whisper naughty things in my ear in that voice." She grabbed him around the nape of his neck and dragged his mouth back down to her throat.

He chuckled darkly into her ear and whispered, "I want to get inside you... do you want me inside you?"

"Uh-huh." She nodded and leaned her head to one side, giving him better access to her throat.

"What part of me do you want buried in you?" he husked and licked the shell of her ear. "This?" He dropped his hips and ground his erection against her thigh. "Or these?" He scraped the points of his fangs over her earlobe and she shuddered and moaned beneath him.

"Dirty witch," he purred and she melted.

"You make me like this." She grabbed his shoulder and rolled, forcing him onto his back and ending up astride his hips. She moaned with the memory of when she had been like this before, naked with him inside her, riding his beautiful cock. Her groin throbbed, hot and damp for him, ready to welcome him back inside. "Gods, I want you."

She made fast work of his shirt buttons and ignored the way he smirked, a flicker of pride in his eyes. Yes, he drove her wild and made her do things she would never have dreamed of doing before meeting him. He didn't have to look so smug about it.

She tore the rest of the dark grey shirt open, sending buttons pinging across the room.

Payne growled at her. "I liked this shirt."

"It was in my way," she said and spread the sides of it, revealing his delicious body. He flexed for her, every muscle rippling and making her ache to touch him. With her mouth. She lowered her head and swept her tongue over his pale hard flesh, savouring the feel of him beneath her. He groaned and tensed again, his hips rising off the mattress to press against hers. She bore down on him, grinding her body along the rigid length of his cock. "Mother earth, you're wearing too many clothes."

He chuckled again. "So are you."

Elissa rose off him and yanked her black top off, freeing her breasts. Payne groaned and she paused to appreciate the hungry way he stared at her, as though he was barely stopping himself from taking command and devouring her.

As though she was beautiful.

Images popped in her head, visions of them naked and entwined, Payne moving against her, making love with her in front of the fire.

She frowned at him, right into his gold and blue eyes. They glowed brightly.

"I thought I warned you about that?"

He smiled sheepishly. "I can't control it sometimes when I look at you... it just takes over..."

"Why don't I react to it the way I do with the other incubi? When they turn on the charm, I feel powerless and as though I want to do those things with them."

His smile faded and he averted his gaze. His hands skimmed up and down her thighs.

"Payne?" She wouldn't let him get away with the silent treatment. She had never had an incubus attempt to use his powers of persuasion on her before Payne, so she had thought perhaps it was a witch thing and that was why she could sense he was attempting to lure her with the visions of them making love. When one of the males in the orgy had tried the same trick, she had wanted to go to him, had felt hungry for him and needy. She had been wrong about Payne and her immunity to his charms. "Is it because you're only part incubus?"

He shook his head.

"Then what is it?" She had a suspicion she knew but she needed to hear him say it.

His steely gaze shifted back to her and he looked as though he was afraid to tell her. He sighed and scrubbed his hands through his hair. "You're my mate."

Elissa stared straight into his eyes, trying to see if he was telling the truth. He had never looked so deadly serious and it sent a shiver through her. When she had announced her plan to come with him, she had said about coming here as his mate, and he had reacted in a bad way. Now she knew why. She had thought perhaps it had had something to do with what that bitch had done to him but it was so much more than that. He had reacted weirdly all those times around her, had challenged incubi males, because she really was his mate.

"Seriously?" She had to check because she was having trouble getting herself to believe it.

He nodded. "I can't control you or read your aura. It's a sure sign... and you make both sides of me insane with a need to claim you."

She tensed. He smiled slightly.

"Don't worry. I won't."

Elissa frowned at him now. Why the heck not? Didn't he want her? An urge to slap him for that rose up inside her but she ignored it, deciding it was safer to glare at him rather than strike him. He was a vampire. He would be able to sense her anger.

He sighed. "Believe me, Witch, I want to... but you don't want to be tied to a fucked up excuse for a male like me."

She didn't? Who the heck was he to decide that for her anyway? He really needed to get over his complex about his dual natures and stop letting it colour his judgement. Couldn't he see in her eyes that she wanted him with all of her heart?

Hadn't everything she had been through with him shown him that she already belonged to him in some way?

She opened and closed her mouth, trying to form a response that would convince him that he was wrong about her. Before she could get it out into the open, he had rolled her onto her back and sucked her left nipple into his mouth, shattering her thoughts and stealing her voice. She groaned and melted into the bed, hungry for more as his cool tongue flicked the bud and then swirled around it. Sparks shot out in all directions from the centre of her breast, electrical currents that lit her up inside. She writhed beneath him, unable to control herself.

Payne groaned and slid his hand over her bare stomach. She raised her hips, encouraging him to continue heading south, towards where she needed him most. He undid her belt with one hand and then worked on her jeans, getting them open without breaking his stride. He circled her nipple with his tongue and then sucked it greedily into his mouth, the pleasure of his caress too much for her. She arched her chest into him, eager for more.

He slipped his hands into her underwear and tore another moan from her throat as his fingers found her moist centre.

"Payne," she whispered, breathless and alive with sensation. She rocked her hips against his fingers, her mind already two steps ahead, imagining his tongue stroking her there and his fingers plundering her body.

Payne reared back and stared down at her, shock written across his face. "What did you just think?"

She blinked, as surprised as he looked. A blush scalded her cheeks. "Um."

Judging by how surprised he looked, he had just got hit by whatever she had been fantasising about, and he really hadn't expected her to be able to project it into his head just as he could project naughty things into hers.

A sudden image of him grasping her hands above her head, pinning them to the mattress as he took her swift and hard, burst into her mind and Payne choked, his eyes shooting wide.

Oh, it was definitely a two-way street.

He growled, grabbed her hands, and pinned them above her head, just as she had imagined. She groaned as he thrust against her, grinding his hard bulge between her legs, teasing her. That hadn't been part of her vision. He had been naked and inside her, not irritatingly clothed.

Elissa wriggled and he tightened his grip on her, giving her a taste of his full strength. Mother earth, it made her hot for him. A shot of lust straight into the vein.

Payne clutched both of her wrists in one hand and worked on his jeans with his other, freeing his cock. He stroked his hand down the length, revealing the crown, and she licked her lips, hungry to taste him. He groaned and sat back, pulling her with him. He stripped out of his shirt, tossing it onto the floor, and his boots and socks followed. He made quick work of his jeans and underwear and then tackled hers. Elissa tried to help but only got in his way, earning a dark growl from him. He yanked her shoes off and then pulled her jeans so hard that she ended up flat on her back again.

He threw her clothes onto the floor and she lay bare on the bed, excitement flowing through her, her mind darting all over the place, imagining the possibilities. Payne knelt before her, gloriously nude and rock hard. Her gaze lingered on his hard cock and she nibbled her lower lip, hungry for another taste of him. He grabbed her arm and pulled her to him, forcing her onto her knees. He rose to his at the same time, tangled his fingers in her long hair and guided her towards his hard length.

Elissa flicked her tongue over the crown of his cock. His groan was so low and guttural that she throbbed, moisture flowing from her as thoughts of him sinking his hard shaft into her core flooded her mind. He groaned again and she took him into her mouth, easing down him until the soft head of his erection touched the back of her throat. She propped herself up on one hand, kneeling before him, and rolled his balls with her other one. His grip on her hair tightened and he groaned as he controlled her movements, making her suck his cock. She tugged on his balls and his groan came out as a short bark of pleasure. She glanced up the length of his body at his face and he looked down at her, his eyes drenched in desire as he watched her sucking him. The blue and gold in his irises swirled, brightening by degrees until his eyes glowed again. The markings that curved over the front of his shoulders turned shades of cobalt and yellow, shimmering like his eyes.

He swallowed and moaned, kept moving her mouth on him, thrusting gently now, easing himself into her. She sucked hard on each withdraw, squeezing his balls at the same time, giving him that hint of pain that seemed to enhance his pleasure. His eyes brightened again and his markings glowed in the same fierce colours.

He moved his hand to the top of her head and stopped her, holding her away from him. She got the message. Either she gave him a moment to calm down or she was going to push him over the edge. Elissa wriggled and stared at his cock, gaze following the thick ridge that ran down the underside, from his balls to the crown. Sense told her not to play with fire. Desire said to throw the rules out of the window and lick him.

She ran her tongue over the head of his cock.

Payne growled, the sound feral and pained, and suddenly she was on her back, her hands locked together by one of his, pinned to the pillows above her head. He knocked her knees apart and she gasped as he entered her, swift and brutal, burying himself as deeply as he could go. He groaned and his grip on her wrists tightened, verging on painful.

"Payne?" She tried to get him to look at her but he had his eyes closed, his face contorted in pleasure. He eased out slowly and then thrust inside again, and a spark of pleasure shot along her thighs and through her belly, erasing her trepidation. He clutched her wrists in one hand, holding her at his mercy, and held his weight off her with his other.

She moaned with each deep plunge of his cock into her body, each delicious invasion that sent shivers tripping over her skin. She tried to buck against him, wanting more. He snarled at her, vicious and dark, and grabbed her hip with his free hand, settling all of his weight on her wrists. Elissa flinched.

"It hurts." She wriggled beneath him, trying to get her hands free. "Payne?"

He pulled her hips off the bed and thrust into her, harder now, sending fire rushing through her blood each time his pelvis hit her clitoris. She moaned and lost herself again, drowning in the mind-blowing feel of him moving inside her, his long strokes hitting her in just the right place to have her squirming beneath him, clenching and reaching for more.

He grunted and quickened his thrusts and she closed her eyes and arched up to meet him, unable to stop herself. He moaned, the sound wanton and erotic, and she groaned with him, her breathing accelerating in time with his pace. He pumped her hard and she could feel his desperation flowing through her, echoing within her. She pressed her heels into the mattress and worked her body against his, frantic and needy, lost in her passion and arousal.

"More," she breathed and Payne lengthened his strokes, driving her insane with each long plunge of his cock into her core. Gods, she needed more. It wasn't enough.

She flicked her eyes open and stared up at his face, using the sight of his pleasure to heighten her own and push her onwards towards climax. Her belly tightened, heat coiling there, ready to explode at any moment. She needed it. She reached for it. He groaned with each tightening of her body around his, pumping harder, taking her higher. Her thighs quivered, release almost within her reach. Close. Closer. She panted, rocking against him, riding his cock as he thrust into her, his pelvis striking her clitoris.

Elissa cried out as pleasure exploded through her, sending her legs trembling and heart racing. Her limbs slackened and she could no longer support her weight. Payne's grip on her hip tightened, holding her in place as he thrust into her, not slowing his pace.

He pressed her hands harder against the mattress, the pain of his grip overshadowing her pleasure. He groaned and increased his pace.

"You're hurting again."

His eyes finally opened and a flicker of fear shot through her, cold realisation dawning at the back of her mind.

They weren't only gold and blue now. Red shone like a corona around his elliptical pupils, his vampire side emerged to join in. He bore his fangs at her and a stab of panic joined the fear. He purred.

Now she knew why he avoided sexual encounters and why he had warned her not to push him.

His incubus side drove him to create pleasure that he could feed on but his vampire nature drew the most pleasure from fear. Each time she felt a touch of fear, he reacted as though she had given him a hit a pure bliss. She tried to calm herself, telling herself that he would never harm her so her fear lessened, knowing he would be fighting to regain control over his hungers and needed her help, but it was impossible. Fear flooded her and he grunted and moaned, his face twisting in pleasure and his grip on her increasing in strength. She had to calm down for his sake as well as her own. The more she feared, the darker his urges would become, his need to feed driving him to terrify her.

"Payne, listen to me," she whispered, focusing on him. She trusted this man. He had warned her not to push him and that he might kill her if she did, and she had still recklessly shoved him over the edge.

Red blazed in the centre of his eyes, surrounded by shimmering gold and blue. He dropped her hip and slid his arm beneath her. She bit her lip to stifle her need to cry out when he grabbed her hair and tugged her head back. He stared down at her through those mesmerising eyes, his body moving against hers, giving her pleasure laced with pain and fear. She tried to stifle her desire, tried not to feel aroused as he thrust into her, deep and fast, bringing her towards another climax.

His lips parted.

No fangs. Did that mean he was more in control than she thought? Could she bring him back before things went too far?

She opened her mouth and he claimed her lips, kissing her so fiercely that she couldn't breathe and couldn't think. She could only feel and submit to him. As she relaxed, his grip on her wrists loosened but not enough for her to get free. She forgot her need to struggle and lost herself again, swamped by the delicious sensations racing through her, evoked by the feel of him moving inside her and kissing the breath from her lungs.

He reared back, slamming deep into her, and she cried out as she came again, her body throbbing around his. His lips curved into a dark smile, revealing fangs this time, and he stared down at her, possessing her with his hungry heavy-lidded eyes that spoke of intense pleasure and satisfaction.

His grip on her wrists tightened again.

Elissa panicked.

She hadn't cast her spell.

She focused on the words, getting the first few out, but then he shattered her chances by striking hard and sinking his fangs into her throat. His body shuddered against hers and a third climax came upon her so swiftly that it rocked her to her core, causing her to tremble along with him. She breathed hard, struggling to catch her breath, hazy from head to toe as he drank from her throat, his body buried deep within hers.

No.

Panic welled up again and she bucked against him, feeling him throbbing within her.

"No!" she shrieked and he stilled, frozen against her, inside her.

He was still for long minutes. She could feel her blood leaking from her, spilling from between his lips.

He disappeared and she shook as she pushed herself up onto her elbow to see where he had gone, her right hand covering the ragged marks on her throat.

Payne stalked around the room, grabbing his clothes and dressing. He was shaking too, trembling so badly that it took him several attempts to get his underwear on. He growled, a noise born of frustration and pain, turned and slammed his fist into the wall above the fireplace. The green plaster cracked and fell away, revealing stone beneath. Blood trickled down from his knuckles and she swore she could feel his pain and his panic, his fear as he stood there with his fist against the wall, his back heaving with his breaths.

"Payne?" she whispered, unsure what she was going to say. He didn't look at her. "Payne? I should have stopped... I shouldn't have pushed you."

He shoved away from the wall and pulled his shirt on, not bothering to heal his hand or lick the blood away. It soaked through the sleeve of his grey shirt and dripped to the floor as he tugged his jeans on and buttoned them. He wiped the back of his clean hand across his bloodied mouth, the action rough and vicious.

She cast a small spell, one to help her feel him more clearly.

He stopped and stared at her, his eyes brimming with hurt and remorse, and self-loathing. "It wasn't your fault... I... I... can't do this. I can't look at you... I never meant for this... I never wanted to hurt you... I only wanted... I just... I'm sorry."

"Don't," she said and moved to kneel on the bed, reaching for him. She didn't want him to teleport out of her life because she had failed to keep her end of the bargain. She had said she would use a spell to stop him and she knew it was the only reason he had agreed to make love with her, and then she had pushed him over the edge. She hated what had happened to her, knew that he was partly to blame too, but she didn't want him blaming himself and only himself. They had entered into this together and she could have stopped him. She should have stopped herself. "Talk to me... please, Payne?"

He looked lost again, as uncertain as she felt. His eyebrows furrowed and he swallowed hard, his eyes holding hers and overflowing with pain and fear. His hands shook at his sides, visibly trembling, and she knew that he could see her shaking too, that she looked as confused, afraid and broken as he did.

"Elissa..."

Someone knocked at the door. He stared at her for a few seconds and then shoved his fingers through his hair, went to the door and opened it.

"Arnaud wishes to see you now." A male voice drifted into the room and Elissa gathered the green covers around herself, feeling cold to the bone. She wanted Payne to look at her and tell her that everything was going to be all right and they could work through this, they could deal with it together. She had the terrible feeling that he would leave her without a word or a look instead.

Payne glanced at her, sorrow in his beautiful grey eyes, all trace of gold, blue and red gone from them now.

She held her hand out to him, afraid to hope that he would take it.

Her heart lifted when he turned away from the open door and crossed the room to her. He pressed one knee into the mattress, took her hand and leaned over her. He dropped a kiss on her forehead and lingered there, his lips pressing against her skin and his hand shaking in hers.

"Don't go anywhere... please? Give me a second chance... please, Elissa?" he whispered hoarsely against her skin and she nodded, raised her hand and managed to stroke his cheek before he pulled away.

He smiled tightly, turned around and walked out of the door, closing it behind him.

Elissa sat in the middle of the bed, cold and afraid, feeling her connection to the earth slowly severing. What had she done? She swallowed and tears filled her eyes. She closed them, causing the hot drops to spill down her cheeks, and drew her knees to her chest, her ears ringing and head spinning as she thought about what had happened and felt herself weakening.

Her coven would know what she had done. They would feel themselves weakening too. It wouldn't be long before they hunted her down. Would Payne protect her when they came? Would he still see her as his mate now? She prayed to the earth and the sky that he would, because she had just turned her back on her world and she wouldn't survive what was to come without him at her side, protecting her as fiercely as he had that day they had met.

The air shifted.

Someone had teleported into the room.

"Payne?" she said, sure that he had returned to her, unable to remain away when he could probably feel her jumbled emotions through the connection between their blood, and that he would reassure her now that everything was going to be fine. She opened her eyes and lifted her head, and stared at the male before her. Dark blond hair, stony grey eyes, but this wasn't the man her heart was pining for. Her voice turned cold and anger curled through her, causing her magic to stir and awaken. "Arnaud."

If he was here, did that mean he had lured Payne away, ensuring she would be alone?

"When my aide told me of my grandson suddenly showing up with a woman he claimed was his mate, and he described you both to me, I had thought perhaps it would be you," he said in a glacial tone and neatened the cuffs of his dark red shirt, his eyes on them, as though he couldn't bring himself to look at her.

Elissa tucked the covers around her, shielding her nudity from his eyes, and glared at him. Magic rose to her fingertips, darker than any spell she had ever dared to call before. She had thrown her life away. She might as well use the black arts now that her coven was already coming to kill her. Any punishment they chose to inflict upon her for using forbidden magic couldn't be worse than death.

"What do you want?" she said, trying her hardest to sound unafraid when she was shaking right down to her bones.

Arnaud straightened, his broad frame and height imposing when she was sitting. His grey gaze raked over her and the gold and cobalt in it brightened, swirling iridescently like Payne's eyes had so many times when he had been looking at her. Unlike Payne, this man didn't fill her with a desire to blush when he gazed upon her. He filled her with fear and disgust.

"You smell like sex... like my grandson. Don't tell me the little witch didn't heed the cautionary tale of her sister and allowed a demon to climax while inside her?"

Her skin crawled as he lowered his gaze to her hips and she moved her hands there, revealing the orbs of black that lazily drifted around them.

He smiled and raised his eyes to meet hers.

"What do you want?" she repeated.

"I would like to know what you are doing with my grandson." He looked genuinely concerned and then darkness crossed his face, his eyes brightening at the same time. "And why you are here?"

"Payne promised to help me bring Luca home." It wasn't a lie, not wholly. Payne had promised to help her bring what she had wanted home, but he didn't know that the item she had come to retrieve was in fact her nephew, and a relation of his.

Arnaud snorted. "The boy is mine."

"I swore to raise him and protect him... he is mine." She moved to kneel, bringing herself closer to eye-level with him, unwilling to let him intimidate her.

"Why did you allow my grandson to violate you?" He stared at her, eyes narrowing, glowing now. Why wouldn't he let that one go? She refused to blush as she wanted to and set her jaw, showing him that he wouldn't get an answer to that question. "Did you do it so he would help you... or perhaps you wished to bear the child of a demon too?"

He took a step towards her, his gaze locked on her, assessing her.

Elissa trembled and said the one thing that sprang into her mind. "He is my mate."

Arnaud threw his head back and laughed. Not the reaction she had hoped to gain from him. He snapped his head down and stared straight into her eyes.

"You believe that, don't you? Poor child. No spawn of mine would tie themselves to a witch. Has he told you that you are his mate now and forever, that he will never be with another?"

She shook her head, cold creeping in again.

"He will leave you. He strung you along and made you believe you were special, and now he has you as his plaything... and when he grows bored of you, he will move on... and you will be left at the mercy of your coven."

She knew he was playing on her fears and she told herself not to listen, but her heart didn't heed her. It ached at the thought that he might be right and Payne would leave her as soon as he had the ring from his grandfather. She had given him no reason to stay with her. She had provoked him at every turn, using him to get her here, so she could take Luca home. She was no better than everyone else who had manipulated him or hurt him.

"You know I am right. I see it in your eyes. Come, child, console yourself." He opened his arms to her and she felt the pull, a deep need to go to him and nestle in his arms. She wanted to cry in his embrace and let him comfort her. "I will make you forget my grandson."

Elissa moved to the edge of the bed, nodding in agreement. She wanted to forget Payne and all the hurt he had caused her. She wanted Arnaud to take her in his arms and hold her close to him, making love to her until she no longer remembered his bastard grandson.

Arnaud took her hand and lifted it to his lips, pressing a long kiss to the back of it. She shivered, a hot rush racing through her blood, and stared up into his beautiful eyes.

"Give yourself to me and I will give you his true name, and you can take your revenge."

Elissa froze and pulled back. "No."

She shook her head to clear the fog of desire from it.

"No!" She tried to tug her hand free of his grip. She would never do that to Payne. She would never use his true name against him, never wanted to know it so she couldn't be tempted to betray him just as his love had.

Elissa clawed at Arnaud's hand and froze again. The ring that Payne wanted. The gold band encircled Arnaud's little finger, the rubies set into it sparkling and taunting her. She could get it for him. She grabbed for it. Arnaud snatched his hand away.

"You won't enslave me, little witch." He shoved her hard onto her back on the bed and was on her before she could move. He grabbed her left wrist and she punched him hard with her other fist as he pulled the blanket off her, baring her to him.

He forced her knees apart and she wrestled with him, heart pounding and blood rushing. She fought harder but he was stronger than she was. Too strong.

His free hand went to his trousers.

"I will enslave you."

CHAPTER 14

Payne stood in the middle of the blue room he had waited in with Elissa the night before when they had first arrived, surrounded by books and the sumptuous antique furniture. The dark-haired male who had escorted him down to the reception room had disappeared, leaving Payne alone to mull over what he had done. He had buttoned as much as he could of his shirt and tucked the rest into his jeans, trying to conceal the fact it had lost half of its buttons. He closed his eyes, hating the instant replay of Elissa's wicked smile as she tore it open, passion flaring in her eyes. If only things had remained that way, harmless satisfaction of their desires, rather than taking a sharp downward turn.

Guilt gnawed at his heart and he wanted to head back upstairs to check on Elissa and try to repair the damage he had done, not that it was possible. He had condemned her. He had done his best to resist, had warned her to stop, but she hadn't listened and he hadn't been able to keep control of himself.

He scrubbed a hand over his hair, raking the blond strands back, tugging at them until it hurt. Pain that he deserved but that wasn't enough. He should suffer a thousand times worse for what he had done tonight, to her. He had tried so hard to claw back control, had almost succeeded once or twice, horrified by what he was doing, by how far gone he had been in that moment. The combination of twin hungers, the constant thrum of sexual energy in the air of the mansion, and Elissa's actions and his deep need for her had conspired to strip away all sense of control and push him firmly over the edge, beyond any hope of salvation.

His stomach turned over and over, churning like a tempestuous ocean. How could he have done that to her? He should have forced her to stop somehow, or fought harder against the urges that had consumed him. He should have done something other than destroy her.

He found no consolation in the fact that she had said she would use a spell to protect herself. He couldn't shift the blame to her, not this time. It lay at his feet. She had trusted him, had given herself to him despite her fears, and he had ruined her.

He was a monster.

And he wasn't sure whether she would stay as he had asked.

Part of his heart felt certain that when he returned to their room, he would find that she had left already, unable to bear the sight of him, unwilling to hear what he had to say.

He still wasn't sure exactly what that was.

Deep in his soul, he knew what he wanted to ask of her, but he feared that she would reject him. The thought of her turning on him as others in his life had, scorning him and telling him that he was a monster and she hated him, chilled his blood and froze his breath in his lungs. He struggled for air, his throat closing, and barely stopped himself from teleporting back to their room.

The door opened and he steadied himself, unwilling to show weakness in front of anyone, especially his grandfather.

The man in the doorway looked nothing as Payne had expected. He was middle-aged in appearance and had short fair hair, but he didn't resemble Payne in any way, and he certainly didn't resemble his mother.

The male stepped into the room, a forced smile plastered on his handsome face, and held out his hand. The cuff of his black shirt drew back as he extended his hand towards Payne, revealing the fae markings tracking along the underside of his forearm.

Payne looked at them.

He didn't recognise any of the symbols.

"You're not my grandfather." He stepped back from the male and held his blue gaze. "Where is my grandfather?"

Before he had finished that question, flashes of Elissa burst into his mind and her panic flooded the lingering connection between them in his blood. His heart thawed and caught fire. His fangs elongated and his eyes switched, his pupils narrowing and stretching as crimson shot through his irises. He snarled at the sight of her with another man.

His grandfather.

Elissa was in danger.

Payne focused on their room and teleported. He landed hard in the middle of the bedroom and his heart turned over when he saw her on the bed, pinned beneath a male. He roared and launched forwards, grabbing the back of the large male's dark red shirt. Elissa kicked and shrieked, the terrified sound driving Payne deep into a killing rage. He pulled the male off her and threw him across the room, sending him crashing into one of the green velvet armchairs. It tipped back and slammed into the wooden floor.

He turned his back on Elissa, facing his opponent, and spread his legs, setting his feet shoulder width apart. He growled low in his throat, threatening the male now getting to his feet, keeping his focus and his eyes locked on him so he couldn't get the jump on Payne.

Elissa moved behind him, scrabbling across the bed, her sobs punctuating the heavy silence. Her fear filled the whole room and he snarled, mind black with the urge for violence and his rage. His mate was hurt, afraid. He would remove the source of her fear and protect her.

His grandfather found his feet and Payne didn't give him a chance to attack. He launched himself at him, taking him back down and shattering a wooden side table in the process. His grandfather grabbed one of the broken mahogany legs and swung at Payne as he moved astride his legs, pinning him down. Payne growled and blocked it with his left arm, the pain of the blow not registering in the haze of his lust for violence and retribution, and smashed his right fist into the male's face, cracking his jaw.

Arnaud retaliated, disappearing from beneath Payne. Payne's senses blared a warning and he rolled forwards. The wooden leg plunged into the floorboards, punching a hole where Payne's heart would have been. He snarled, got to his feet, and flexed his fingers as his claws extended. His grandfather stood between him and Elissa, brandishing the makeshift stake. Payne assessed his surroundings, eyes darting and searching for any weapons he could use if it came to it. He didn't want to rely on anything manmade, but it was nice to have a backup plan.

Elissa muttered something dark and unholy, and a black blast shot from her trembling hands and slammed into Arnaud's back, sending him flying across the room towards Payne.

Payne ducked and threw himself forwards, under his grandfather, and rolled to his feet in front of Elissa. Tears streaked her pink cheeks and swam in her eyes, and the way they met his, the need that shone in them, filled him with an urge to gather her in his arms. He wanted to go along with that and give her what she needed, wanted to hold her and whisper that she was safe now and he would never allow anyone to harm her ever again because she was his to protect, but now wasn't the time.

Arnaud grumbled and got to his feet at the other end of the room. Payne turned to face him. His grandfather brushed the plaster dust off his dark crimson shirt and fixed him with a black look. He had lost his weapon when Elissa had blasted him with magic.

Payne flexed his fingers again and drew in a deep steadying breath. His blood screamed for him to kill this man for what he had tried to do to his mate but he fought to tamp down that black urge, knowing that if he succumbed to it that he would have the whole den after him. Elissa would be in more danger, and he had already put her in the path of angry witches. He didn't need to throw enraged incubi into the mix too.

Elissa moved behind him. His grandfather stood before him, eyes swirling darkest gold and blue. If Payne could see his fae markings, they would be as black and red as his own were.

"Are you alright?" he said thickly to Elissa, his voice tight and dark, gravelly.

"I think so... I don't know... I'm scared."

Payne already knew that but her admission tightened his chest and darkened his heart. He would kill his grandfather for daring to touch her. No, he wouldn't. He had to keep a level head. He would get what they had come here for and then they would get the hell away from this place and he would never see his wretched grandfather again.

The vampire side of him snarled at that, outraged that he was planning to leave this male alive. He had dared to assault his mate. He had frightened her, threatened her, hurt her. He deserved nothing less than death. A slow, terrible, painful death.

Payne growled, his top lip curling back to flash his fangs at Arnaud.

The incubus stared him down, no trace of fear showing on his face, but Payne could feel it in his blood, a rich tang that hung in the air and enticed him to sever his control and unleash Hell on this disgusting beast before him.

He drew in another breath, deeper this time, and tried to expel his darker needs, focusing on the woman behind him and his desire to protect her. If he fought again with his grandfather, there was no telling how it would turn out. He had ended up with Arnaud close to her once already. If it happened again, Payne had no doubt that the male would use Elissa as a shield. He couldn't let that happen. He had to be Elissa's shield against this man. He had to protect her.

"It's okay now, Sweetheart. I won't let him near you." He kept his back to Elissa but reached behind him. A comforting rush of heat streaked through him when she placed her delicate hand in his and he closed his fingers, gently holding it and feeling her trembling. His heart took her quick response as a good sign, a gift of hope that when all this was over, he wouldn't be alone in this world.

"My grandson, I presume?" Arnaud straightened to his full height and stared across the room at him, accents of gold and blue swirling in his dark grey eyes.

Payne had to wonder how he could doubt they were related when they looked so alike. Was this what he would have looked like by now if it weren't for his vampire genes? He was aware that his dominant vampire side slowed his aging, so he looked far younger than most incubi his age.

He raised his other arm, revealing the markings that tracked along his forearm. Arnaud's gaze dropped to them and narrowed. That reaction wasn't only because his markings revealed Payne to be his grandson. It was because Payne's markings were coloured by hues of black and darkest red, a sign of the fury he held just below the surface, the need to resort to violence and bloody his claws.

"He has the ring," Elissa whispered and moved closer to him. She clutched his arm in one hand and pointed to Arnaud with the other.

Payne looked down at his grandfather's hands. The man only wore one ring and it was gold and red, and on his little finger.

He held his hand out. "Give it to me."

Arnaud shook his head. "I don't think so. The ring belongs to me."

Payne released Elissa's hand and stared the man down. "I said give it to me."

He didn't give his grandfather a chance to respond this time. He teleported right in front of him and snatched his hand before he could react. Arnaud wrestled with him but Payne's vampire genes gave him power and strength far beyond his grandfather's grasp and he easily twisted Arnaud's arm around. Arnaud's only choice was to fall to his knees to avoid Payne breaking his arm and Payne used that moment to yank the ring from his finger.

He released his grandfather and backed towards Elissa, placing the ring on his little finger at the same time. Arnaud stood and stared at him, murder shining in his eyes. Payne knew he wore the same dark look.

"I want to kill you," Payne growled low, his eyes locked on his grandfather's. "One wrong move and I will. You dare to look at my mate and I won't be able to stop myself. I will kill you."

A soft gasp sounded behind him and he glanced over his shoulder at Elissa where she sat in the middle of the four-poster bed, the green sheets wrapped around her. She had her hands against her chest and the heat in her eyes struck him hard, causing his heart to skip a beat and thump heavily against his ribs.

Had she doubted that he saw her as his mate now, his forever?

He would have to make his intentions clearer to her later, so she would understand that he was never letting her go and that he belonged to her as much as she now belonged to him.

"Do you know the location of what you're looking for now?" he said to her and she shook her head. He turned back to his grandfather, crossed the room to him, and grabbed the front of his red shirt. He twisted the material in his fist and dragged Arnaud towards him. "Where is your room?"

Arnaud stared at him in stony silence.

"I said, where is your room? You would do well to answer me this time. I am a man of very little patience and I'm itching for an excuse to draw blood." Payne flashed his fangs.

"The next floor up, at the far end of the east wing."

The other end of the house to where they were now. Could they make it there, retrieve what Elissa had come here for, and get out before Arnaud alerted the entire mansion and sent every incubus after them?

He couldn't teleport there. It was difficult to teleport anywhere unfamiliar, not without risking ending up in a bad way.

Elissa slipped off the bed behind him. Arnaud's swirling blue and gold gaze slid to her. Payne roared at the sight of desire in his grandfather's eyes, dark twisted hungers that snapped what little hold he had managed to retain over his urge to spill blood.

"I warned you not to look at her." Payne growled, pushed Arnaud backwards and swiped his claws across his throat.

Crimson flowed from the deep slashes, spilling down his neck and soaking into his shirt, darkening the already red material.

It drenched Payne's hand and he released the male. Arnaud collapsed to his knees, gasping as he tried to cover his throat to stem the bleeding. Too late. Payne glared down at him, towering over him, feeling no remorse over his actions. He watched the blood flow from between Arnaud's fingers, saw his eyes return to grey and the flicker of life in them die, and turned away as he fell.

Elissa stared at him, eyes wide and horrified, her skin as pale as moonlight.

"Come," Payne said as he crossed the room to her, wiping his hand on his jeans to clean the blood away. He held his other hand out to her. "We must leave."

"You killed him." Her beautiful silvery eyes flickered between Arnaud and Payne, the shock in them not subsiding.

"I warned him," Payne said on a dark snarl, unable to contain his anger. "I told him not to look at you and he did just that."

"You wanted him dead though... for your mother... for you."

"Yes." He wouldn't lie to her about that. He had wanted Arnaud dead. "But I did not intend to kill him... I would have let him live in order to protect you, so others wouldn't come after us."

"Us?" She almost smiled.

His heart missed another beat. "Us... I swear I will not allow anything to happen to you, Elissa. I condemned you with my actions and I will take responsibility and protect you."

Her face fell and she looked away and busied herself with dressing, tugging on her black halter-top and jeans.

He had said something wrong. Was she angry because he had said he was taking responsibility for what he had done to her, rather than saying that he desired to protect her because he felt something for her and she was his mate? He hadn't said such a thing because he wasn't sure she was ready to hear it, not yet.

"Come," he said again and held his hand out to her. She took it and stepped into his arms. He focused on the floor above, able to teleport to the corridor there and give them a head start. When they had materialised, Elissa pushed out of his arms and raced along the hallway, heading towards the far end.

Whatever Arnaud had taken from her, it was important to her and she wanted it back.

Payne ran behind her, his senses sweeping the rooms, searching for trouble. Some of the bedrooms were occupied but most of the people in them seemed busy judging by the rapid heartbeats and moans he could hear.

Elissa stopped at the far end of the corridor and looked back at him. "Which one?"

Payne slowed to a walk and sniffed, focusing on his grandfather's scent so he could follow it to the right room. He stopped outside a door one room from the end of the hall. "This one."

Elissa went to open it and he grabbed her arm. "What?"

Payne focused on the other side of the door. "Someone is in there."

Arnaud's current lover?

Elissa broke free of him and burst into the room, sobs escaping her. Not fear or sorrow. He couldn't sense such emotions in her as she ran towards the bed, blocking his view of it. She felt happy.

She rounded the bed and Payne's eyes widened as she peeled away the dark blue covers and gathered a small boy who looked no older than six in human years into her trembling arms.

This was the item she had lost?

It couldn't be hers. Payne could sense the boy was an incubus. No markings covered what he could see of the boy's arms beyond the short sleeves of his charcoal grey t-shirt but they would emerge in a few years, revealing his lineage. Payne didn't need to see it to know it would be like his own.

His scruffy sandy hair was evidence enough.

"Who does the boy belong to?" he said and stepped into the room.

Elissa looked up at him, her eyes bright with affection even though tears lined her dark lashes. Her chestnut hair fell around her shoulders and the boy in her arms nuzzled it, reached up and sleepily buried his small hand into the wavy locks. His black loose bottoms blended into her halter-top as he curled up against her and murmured something in his sleep.

"He is mine now... he was my sister's. She gave birth to him and had raised him in secret, moving from one town to the next, forever on the run until the coven finally found her and executed her. I kept my promise to raise him in her stead and I had managed to keep him hidden, but then his father tracked him down." She held the boy closer to her and looked down at him, and Payne could see the love in her eyes as well as feel it in the remnants of her blood in his body.

He wished she would look at him like that, while feeling emotions so warm and beautiful.

Payne looked at the sleeping innocent in her arms. They were related. His grandfather's son. His uncle. That didn't feel right as he looked at the boy, so much younger than he was, new to this dark world and unaware of just what he would become when he matured. A witch had given birth to him, a human, making him a full-blooded incubus, not a half-breed like Payne. The boy would need protecting and teaching. He would need love and Elissa looked as though she would give it to him unconditionally.

He ached inside with the need for her to give that to him too.

"Thank you, Payne," she whispered and looked up at him through her eyelashes.

He shrugged it off. "We have to go."

"Where?" Her voice shook now and he knew what she was thinking.

"I will take you somewhere you will be safe and I can protect you." He was risking a lot by taking her to Vampirerotique but it was the only place he knew and he would only stay there long enough to figure out somewhere else to take her. He would find a safe home for her and the boy.

She rounded the bed and the sight of her struck him hard. She looked beautiful as she carried the boy, gazing upon the sleeping child with love and happiness.

Jealousy coiled in Payne's heart, striking deep with poisoned fangs.

He closed his eyes and took hold of her arm, unable to see her without feeling she was never going to give him what he needed from her and that as soon as they were away from here, she would leave with the boy and he would never see her again. She wouldn't want to keep the child around him. He was barely mate material, let alone father material, and an erotic theatre was no place to raise a child.

Payne focused and teleported them.

Right onto the black stage of the theatre in the middle of a performance. Fuck.

He must have been thinking about what it would be like for the boy to grow up around the erotic shows and got his coordinates skewed.

The whole theatre froze and the combined focus of over two hundred vampires shifting to him and then to Elissa and the boy sent him off the deep end.

Payne roared at them all.

Red bled over his vision.

The two male and two female performers on stage broke apart, crimson eyes on Elissa. Payne growled a warning at them and then things took a severe downward turn. One of the males moved. Payne tried to go for a flesh wound but the thought of Elissa coming to harm, the thought of someone hurting the boy, had him automatically aiming higher. He swiped his claws in a direct arc across the male's throat and thankfully the male had fast reactions.

Victor.

Payne hazily recognised the shaven-headed immense elite male.

His claws caught him on the shoulder, digging deep and ploughing through his flesh. Blood spilled fast and thick from the wound. A female shrieked, not on the stage but in the audience. The other male on the stage growled and bared his fangs.

Payne lost it.

He barrelled into the male, taking him down, and punched him hard. The heady scent of blood saturated the air. Elissa's rapid heartbeat filled his ears, driving him on, urging him to maim and kill, to protect her and her youngling.

A familiar female scent popped into the myriad of smells. Succubus.

"Payne?" Andreu's thickly accented voice reached his ears.

Payne shot backwards, growling and snarling at the dark-haired Spaniard, baring his fangs at the same time as he stretched his bloodied arms out, shielding his female.

Andreu moved a step towards him and Chica held him back, her black hair wild and as ruffled as Andreu's hair, and their clothing too. Half of the buttons on Andreu's black tailored shirt were undone and the tail hung out of his equally dark trousers. Chica's strapless purple corset was wonky and her legs were as bare as her feet beneath her short black layered skirt.

They smelled of sex.

Payne growled low again, hunger blasting through him, twin urges, needs he couldn't deny. The smell of sex and blood filled him with a need to feed, mingling with his need to protect, driving him deeper into his instincts.

"Payne isn't right," Chica said and he bore his fangs at her, his focus locking on her now. Weak female. He snarled and the red spots across his vision were joined by blue and gold. "There's something off about him."

He moved his feet further apart and lowered himself, breathing hard, his focus diverted by the noises and rapid heartbeats surrounding him. Victor's blood spoke to him, luring him into feeding his hunger for it. He wasn't alone now. A female was with him. Clothed in a crimson dress that matched her flame red hair.

She would taste sweeter.

"Payne, talk to us... tell us what is wrong," Andreu said but the words grated in Payne's ears and he struggled to make sense of them.

Payne growled his reply but not in English. Panic shot through him, sending a hot prickly wave across his skin.

Chica released Andreu and walked forwards across the black stage. His focus shifted entirely to her. She wouldn't taste sweet and he didn't want her near him. He didn't want her near his female and her youngling.

He snarled a warning at her.

She didn't heed it. She kept edging towards him. Andreu spoke again, the noise indistinct. Light burst across his eyes from his right. Doors slammed. More scents joined the maddening mixture of them swirling in his mind and his lungs. Stronger scents.

He knew those males.

Payne lifted his hands and pressed his palms to his temples, growling as he tried to remember them. The red haze of fury clouded his mind and he couldn't remember anything, couldn't feel anything other than an insatiable lust for violence.

Chica spoke to him. Her words were strange and confusing, a language he had never fully learned but understood perfectly in the midst of his rage.

"Your markings," she said and he looked at them briefly, seeing the swirling hues of gold, blue and deepest pink. "You have a mate... is this your mate?"

She took another step closer. Payne roared at her. Andreu was instantly between them, shielding her. Payne edged back a step, closer to someone behind him. Someone who meant a lot to him.

Chica swam out of focus and then back again as she spoke from behind her male. "Is this your mate, Payne?"

Payne clawed his hair back with both hands, his head spinning as he fought to make sense of everything that was happening. He growled and squeezed his hands against the sides of his head. He couldn't think over the rush of blood in his ears. His breathing accelerated. Flashes of a beautiful female with flowing chestnut hair and striking silver-grey eyes punctuated the red haze in his mind. He saw himself above her, inside her, biting her, feeling the euphoria of that dual connection and her flowing into him. The taste of her blood was still strong on his tongue and their connection still had hold of his heart and his mind.

Something soft settled on his back, pressing between his shoulder blades and against his backside, spreading warmth across his skin and carrying light into his heart.

He stilled, his fury fading with each second she touched him, with each bit stronger the connection between them grew. Her scent enveloped him and her steady heartbeat replaced the rush of blood in his ears.

"Payne?" Her gentle voice stirred his soul, bringing it up from the darkness to the light, soothing away his fear and his rage, and lifting the red haze from his mind.

He turned slowly to face her and she looked up at him, no trace of fear, anger or disgust in her beautiful eyes. They shone with warmth and understanding, with affection even though he knew what she saw stood before her, a wild and lost male, a broken and vicious man.

"Everything is fine, Payne. You don't have to protect me from these people." She smiled at him and then looked down, and his eyes fell there too, following her gaze to the boy cradled in her arms. "You don't have to protect us."

He raised his eyes to hers again.

Bewitch

"Come back to me, Payne." Her eyes darted between his and he could sense her desire to touch him.

He wanted that too. He stepped up to her, leaned down and rested his heavy head on her slender shoulder, needing to feel her and smell her, and know that she was here with him, safe and sound.

He wasn't sure how long he remained there, weak and tired, confused about everything and feeling so uncertain. Elissa didn't move. She stayed with him, her cheek resting against his, sometimes whispering soothing things to him. He slowly pieced himself back together, tamping down his anger and regaining control. It helped that someone made the audience leave. He wasn't sure who.

The performers left too, but some vampires remained, staring at him, patiently waiting for an explanation.

Elissa pressed a kiss to his cheek and the boy stirred in her arms. Payne drew back to check on him. He slept still. Payne was surprised he hadn't woken yet but when he looked into Elissa's eyes and saw them twinkling like diamonds, he knew why the child still slumbered. She was using her magic to keep him under, protecting him from this dark place that Payne had brought them to.

"I'm sorry," he whispered, voice hoarse and low.

"You were only trying to protect us." She smiled at him, relieving the ache in his heart, and then tiptoed. Payne met her halfway, stealing a kiss from her. He had never needed anything as fiercely as he needed this kiss and the sliver of reassurance that it conveyed to his heart. Perhaps he could fix things after all. Perhaps Elissa would consent to be his mate.

"Are you going to introduce us?" Chica's bright voice filled the theatre and Payne looked over his shoulder at her and Andreu.

And Sera. When had she arrived? She stood at the side of the stage, her blonde hair tied in a neat ponytail, wearing a short black dress.

Antoine and Snow were present too, standing below him at the front of the stalls. He didn't dare look at them. He could feel Antoine's anger and knew the powerful aristocrat would be having words with him later about interrupting a show and scaring away customers.

And bringing a witch and a child to the theatre.

It was the only place he could have taken her.

It was the only place he could call home.

"Elissa," Elissa introduced herself, stepping around Payne, her hand still against the boy's forehead, keeping him asleep. "And this is Luca."

Luca.

Payne looked down at the boy in her arms. Not his real name. Payne knew that instinctively. Because they were related? He wasn't sure how it worked but he had heard that relations couldn't use names against each other.

Antoine leaped up onto the stage. He adjusted the cuffs of his crisp dark silver shirt. Payne couldn't remember ever witnessing Antoine dressed any way other than impeccably in expensive tailored shirts and dark trousers, coupled with Italian leather shoes. He was the total opposite of his older brother Snow, who favoured pairing tight black t-shirts with equally as tight black jeans and army boots. That was, when he bothered to wear more than just his jeans. The immense male had no qualms about roaming around Vampirerotique dressed in only his black jeans, wearing them slung low around his hips.

Sera came forwards and joined Antoine, her sparkling green eyes on the boy rather than her male.

"Is there something you may want to tell us?" Antoine said to Payne.

"Yes... I have the ring... it will free Chica of the theatre, but only by binding her to Andreu." Payne slipped the ring off his little finger and offered it to her. She bounced forwards and took it from him, her grin wide, and then threw her arms around him and gave him a tight hug.

"I knew you'd come good on your promise. Thank you, Payne. I owe you so much." She squeezed him so tightly he choked and then released him and bounced back to Andreu, holding the ring out to him.

Andreu grinned too and Payne couldn't stop himself from smiling along with them, his heart warmed by the sight of them so happy and proud that he had been able to help them after all.

"No, I meant the boy." Antoine pointed to the sleeping child and looked between him and Payne, back and forth, enough times that his meaning dawned on Payne.

"He isn't mine." Payne looked down at Luca and could understand why Antoine had believed there was a possibility that he was the father. "He is related to me though... but it's a long story."

"The boy and the witch must leave... now."

Payne shot a glare at Snow. The lethal white-haired male stared up at him from the front row of the red velvet stalls, his pale blue eyes ringed with crimson.

"I have to protect them... and that means I need to keep them here until I can find a secure home for them."

"No." Snow frowned and his pupils stretched, turning cat-like, and his fangs extended. "It means you need to get them away from here... now."

Payne froze.

Snow growled.

"We are not alone."

CHAPTER 15

Payne's senses stretched out, screaming in alert. Antoine and Andreu tensed, both males pulling their females close to them. Both females broke out of their arms and readied themselves for a fight. Payne knew if he tried to coddle Elissa she would react in the same way.

Snow leaped up onto the stage, his red eyes scanning the stalls and then the private boxes that lined the walls of the theatre.

Payne couldn't detect what Snow had sensed coming but he tried to prepare himself for it.

Witches or incubi?

Were they coming for Elissa or coming for him?

Either way, he wouldn't allow anything to happen to Elissa or the boy.

He backed towards her, keeping her close.

What was keeping them?

He turned and scanned the stalls, and then froze as the hairs on the back of his neck rose and he caught their scent.

Incubi.

They were here for him. He growled and extended his claws. Five males appeared on the stage and it erupted into pandemonium. Payne tried to remain near Elissa as he fought, dealing with a dark-haired young male wielding a sword. It seemed the incubi had come prepared for the fight, leaving his side at a disadvantage.

Antoine growled at Andreu. "Take care of the females."

Andreu looked as though he was going to protest and then thought the better of it, sticking close to Sera and Chica as he battled a man with long blond hair.

Snow roared and swiped his claws across the throat of a middle-aged dark-haired male, ripping it open. The sight of one of their comrades dying didn't slow the incubi. More of them appeared, among them the two males Payne had met at the mansion. The one who had welcomed them and the one who had pretended to be his grandfather. Antoine threw himself into the fray, taking on two incubi at a time, his movements swift and brutal. Snow fought alongside him, dealing deadly blows and bloodying his hands. His eyes burned crimson.

Payne kept a wary eye on the immense lethal male, unwilling to trust him when the scent of blood was thick in the air. One wrong step and Snow would lose himself to bloodlust.

"Antoine," Payne shouted above the din of the fight and the dark-haired aristocrat's blue eyes met his as he punched a hole through the chest of one of the incubi. Payne caught his opponent with a right hook followed by a swift left uppercut, sending him crashing onto the stage. "Take Snow away from here."

Antoine glanced at Snow. Snow grinned at his enemy, shredding him with his claws, his fangs enormous and bloodied. He was feeding on the incubi. No good would come of this.

Antoine nodded and then his eyes widened. Payne sensed the incubi who had appeared behind him, close to Elissa. He turned, his heart lodging in his throat. Everything moved in slow motion, his actions sluggish. Elissa's beautiful eyes grew enormous and she clutched Luca against her. The blond incubi male brought his sword down, aiming straight at her. Payne lunged forwards, reaching for the male, his blood rushing through his ears again.

Antoine reached them first, shoved Elissa backwards out of harm's way, and tried to evade the strike. The tip of the sword slashed across his chest, slicing through his silver-grey shirt. Red instantly drenched the material.

Snow roared.

Everything sped up then. Payne could only stare as Snow tore through the incubi, ending lives in a split second with claw and fang, spraying blood everywhere and butchering the males.

Sera screamed and ran through the insane fight, ducking under Snow's arm as he swung at an incubus, driving claws deep into his chest and tearing through bone to reach his heart. She dropped to her knees and skidded on the blood, and caught Antoine as he collapsed.

The floor ran red with blood.

Snow stopped in the centre of the carnage, holding a male by his torn throat, threw his head back and roared, the sound deafening.

Silence fell.

Snow turned dark red eyes on Elissa.

Payne growled and moved between them, shielding her. Snow would easily tear through him as he had the other incubi, but Payne would do all that he could to protect her.

Snow's broad chest heaved, his black t-shirt drenched in blood. It rolled down his pale thickly muscled arms and dripped from his fingers. He dropped the body of the incubus and regarded Payne with narrowed eyes.

Payne flicked a glance down to Antoine and Sera. The aristocrat male was bleeding badly but he would live. He only needed time to begin healing, someone to clean the wound and some blood to speed the whole recovery process. Something told him that Snow was too far gone to register that. His brother had been injured and he had gone off the deep end, a beast with only desire for blood and violence, mindless with rage and driven by dark instincts. Not bloodlust. This was something else. Something far more terrible.

Snow lunged at Payne.

Payne brought both arms up and blocked his swipe, taking the hit on his forearms. He cried out as Snow's claws shredded his flesh and then threw all of his remaining strength into his attack, slamming the flats of his hands into Snow's chest and sending him flying across the stage and crashing into the wall on the right of the theatre. He fell in a heap and pushed himself up, and shook his head. Red tainted the white lengths of his overlong hair.

Snow growled and bore his fangs.

Andreu and Chica leaped on him before he could get up, trying to pin him down.

"Snow, listen to me." Chica grabbed his hair and tugged his head up. "Payne is not your enemy. We're good here. You hear me?"

Snow roared and reared up, easily shaking them off him. He stumbled to his feet and loped towards Antoine. Sera stared at him, tears streaking her cheeks.

Snow's eyes verged on black.

They moved to Payne and then Elissa. She gasped and Payne felt her fear in his blood, felt the boy in her arms stir as her strength began to fade, her terror stealing it away. The wounds on Payne's arms throbbed, blood rolling in rivulets down to his palms and dripping to the black stage floor. He shut out the stinging pain and the sense that he was weakening, focusing on protecting Elissa and her youngling. He wouldn't allow Snow near her. He wasn't in any position to fight the larger older male, didn't want things to go down that route, but he had to keep her safe.

"Snow," Antoine whispered, his voice hoarse and laden with pain.

Snow's black eyes fell to his brother. He snarled at Sera and she shuffled backwards, giving him access to Antoine. Payne remained on guard, heart pounding, adrenaline flooding every inch of him, and his claws at the ready.

Snow collapsed to his knees beside Antoine and grasped his hand, rocking back and forth as he murmured words in a foreign tongue. Antoine swallowed hard and opened his pale blue eyes, fixing them on Snow above him. Snow's pale eyebrows furrowed and he bore his fangs. Antoine shook his head a fraction but whatever passed unspoken between them didn't stop his older brother. Snow opened his mouth and bit his own wrist, burying his fangs deep and tearing open his flesh.

He offered it to Antoine.

Antoine shook his head again and sounded weary as he spoke. "I cannot take it."

Snow growled and it tailed off into a whimper, and Payne's grey eyes shot wide when he clawed at his own chest, tearing through his black t-shirt and gouging deep gashes in his flesh.

Antoine grimaced and tried to sit up. Sera rushed to help him, kneeling behind him and supporting his back. With visible effort, Antoine grabbed Snow's wrist.

"No, Snow."

Snow didn't stop. He whined and slashed his arms, his wrists, blood flowing freely. Andreu and Chica grabbed his thickly muscled arms, trying to restrain him. Payne helped them but Snow was too strong. He tried to shake them off, growling and whining, the sound harrowing as it echoed around the theatre.

Antoine grasped Snow's hand and Snow stopped to look at him, a lost expression on his blood-streaked face.

"Calm yourself, Brother," Antoine whispered and swallowed. "You did not do this."

Snow's face twisted in agony and he offered his wrist again, his entire arm drenched in blood now. It pulsed from the lacerations, dripping thick and fast onto the black stage floor.

The corners of Antoine's lips lifted in a pained smile. "I will take it... there is no need to spill more for me."

Snow moved his arm towards his mouth and Antoine closed his eyes and fixed his lips around one of the cuts. From what Payne could tell, he only took a little blood from his brother.

Was he afraid that he would make Snow worse if he took more than a sip?

Payne didn't want to find out the answer to that question. Snow was scary enough as it was. He didn't want to encounter Snow in a darker wilder mood than the one he was in now.

"All the pretty colours... do you see them... Aurora..." Snow rocked, his eyes locked on Antoine, and then tilted his head back and stared at the black ceiling of the theatre, his eyes glazed and face streaked with blood. "Come home with me... we can go together... don't go away."

Antoine looked at Chica, eyes swimming with pain and remorse, with sorrow. She nodded and glanced at Andreu, and he nodded too.

Chica released Snow's arm and laid her palm against his cheek. She moved to kneel beside him and he looked at her, his eyes as black as midnight but soft with trust. Was he aware of what Chica was going to do?

"Take me home," Snow whispered in a low broken voice and his eyebrows furrowed. "Aurora. Prettier than the heavens. Take me there with you."

Chica leaned in and pressed her lips to his, and kissed him.

Snow's arm instantly dropped from Antoine's lips. No one besides their mate or the strongest of males could withstand a succubus's kiss. Snow was strong. How much energy would Chica have to steal to render him unconscious? He wavered, eyelids drooping, and then fell back onto the stage with a heavy thud.

Antoine pushed himself up and grabbed Snow's hand, his distress written across his face and in his scent. He shirked Sera's touch, crawled to his brother and gathered Snow to him, sitting with his arms around his broad shoulders and his face pressed into his bloodied white hair.

Chica leaned over and pressed her ear to Snow's chest, and relief crossed her face.

She sat back and looked around at everyone, and then settled her eyes on Antoine. "He will be alright, but I had to take a lot of energy. When coupled with the amount of blood he lost... I'm not sure how long he will be out."

"The longer the better," Antoine whispered and smoothed Snow's bloodstained brow, brushing the hair from it, his pale blue eyes fixed on him with affection and a touch of fear. "He will need rest to recover from this setback."

Andreu stared at the back of Antoine's head. "Did you know he was capable of this?"

Payne's gaze briefly scanned the carnage strewn across the black boards around them. Snow had torn more than one incubus apart, littering the theatre with their remains. Vampires were notoriously violent when driven into a protective rage, but Snow's actions had been more than that. Payne could recognise signs of a terrible past haunting someone, and whatever had happened in Snow and Antoine's history, had been darker than black and it had wounded the two brothers deeply, especially Snow. Payne had seen the scars on Antoine's body. He could piece things together for himself and knew why Snow had lost it when he had seen Antoine bleeding.

Antoine growled. "He would have been fine... we wouldn't be in this mess... Snow wouldn't be like this if it wasn't for that witch."

"No." Payne placed himself between Antoine and Elissa, struggling to keep his balance on the slippery bloody stage. The lacerations on his forearms stung, blood leaking from the deep gashes, but it wouldn't stop him from fighting to protect her. "You dare blame her for this. I brought her here... I killed their leader... my grandfather. I ruined her... I ruined everything. This is my fault."

Antoine snarled at him, baring his fangs, his eyes blazing red. Sera went to him and wrapped her arms around both him and Snow, whispering soothing words to her lover.

Payne watched him closely, not trusting him.

"Elissa doesn't deserve your anger. She gave us the key to fixing the mess you created, Antoine. It was an incubus who hurt you... but it was you who refused Snow's blood and sent him into some sort of self-harming trance... blame me, if you want, but don't you dare blame her."

This was all his fault. Yet again, he had brought pain to people he cared about when all he ever wanted to do was protect and care for them.

They would all reject him now.

He had to do something to stop that from happening.

"Let me help you with Snow," he said and Antoine scowled at him.

"No."

Sera helped Antoine to his feet and then Andreu tried to help him with Snow. It was ridiculous. Antoine needed blood and rest. He didn't have the strength to lift Snow when he was a dead weight. Chica stepped in and her strain was visible on her face as she tried to teleport them.

"Let me help you." Payne tried again. "Please, Antoine? Let me try to make this right."

Elissa's feelings flowed through the link between their blood and he cursed her for pitying him, for knowing his innermost fears and how terrible he felt, and his crushing need to try to make amends.

"Please?"

Sera whispered to Antoine, her face a picture of concern. Antoine nodded.

Before Payne could take a step towards Snow, Elissa was beside him. He glanced down at her and she lowered the boy, setting his feet on the floor and keeping one arm around his back. She gently laid her free hand on Payne's bloodied left arm and her eyes twinkled.

A hot ache ignited in his bones and he grimaced as the cuts on his forearms stung fiercer than before, burning as she used her magic to seal his wounds. The pain slowly eased and then faded completely, leaving only a peaceful sort of warmth behind. She smiled shakily and he helped her lift the boy back into her arms, and couldn't resist pressing a kiss to her forehead, silently thanking her for easing his pain and for caring about him.

Payne lifted Snow with Andreu's help and looked back at Elissa. He didn't want to leave her here with the others, was afraid that something might happen to her if he did, but he needed to try to make amends, and this was the only way he could think of making things better between him and Antoine. Elissa held his gaze, no trace of fear in her now, her silvery

Bewitch

eyes sparkling like starlight. She was powerful and he knew deep in his heart that she could take care of herself and her youngling if it came down to it, and he would sense if she was in any danger.

"Stay here. I will only be a moment," he said and she nodded.

He teleported both Snow and Andreu to Snow's room and settled the large unconscious male on his bed. Chica appeared with Antoine. Sera burst into the room as Payne was removing Snow's ruined t-shirt. She rushed to Antoine and helped him to the chair beside Snow's steel four-poster bed.

"Take five," she whispered and kissed Antoine. "I'll help get Snow settled."

Payne looked away from them, guilt tearing him apart inside. She was so loving. It made him feel terrible. There was a witch waiting for him downstairs and he wasn't sure what to say to her to make everything all right between them.

Sera was extremely gentle with Snow, carefully stripping him down to his underwear and then helping Payne chain him to the bed. Payne let her deal with the final shackle and rounded the foot of the bed to Antoine. He wasn't sure what to say to him either.

Antoine held his hand out to him. Payne helped him to the bed and held him steady as he settled beside Snow.

"I'll leave," Payne said, his voice steady despite the turbulence churning inside him, pain colliding with fear, stripping away his strength. It was all he could do to make up for tonight. He would leave Vampirerotique and everyone's lives forever. He would go before he brought any more pain to their lives, to people he had come to care about.

He turned to leave.

Antoine caught his wrist, his grip surprisingly strong, and held him firm. "I will expect you back at work tomorrow."

Payne said nothing. He couldn't bring himself to believe that Antoine meant that.

He shirked his grip and took a step towards the door. Andreu was there, blocking the exit. A futile move considering that Payne could teleport. The women stared at him.

Chica poured a glass of blood and handed it to Antoine.

"It wasn't your fault," Sera said, her voice soft and filled with warmth.

Payne closed his eyes and kept his back to her. "It doesn't change what happened. I'm still leaving."

"Why?" Antoine this time and he sounded as though he was losing patience now.

Payne sighed. "I don't belong here."

"Nonsense." Antoine's tone had taken a turn towards dark, a commanding snarl that Payne had heard many times in the months he had been at Vampirerotique, the one that warned to obey or face the consequences. "You are due at work tomorrow and I have something I need you to do tonight."

Payne looked over his shoulder at the dark-haired male.

"Please apologise to the witch and thank her for helping fix what I did to Chica... for undoing some of the pain I have caused. No one here is perfect, Payne, but we can all move past our mistakes and make things better. We are family."

Payne wasn't sure what to say. He stared at Antoine, struggling between rejecting what he had said to protect himself and his heart from a blow that would likely kill him if Antoine was lying and accepting it as the truth. They were family. He did belong here.

He wasn't sure he would ever truly believe that, but he could apologise to Elissa on Antoine's behalf and thank her.

He could make things right with her, and then he would work to make things right with everyone else he had hurt.

He nodded and teleported back to the stage.

Elissa was gone.

CHAPTER 16

Payne focused on Elissa's scent and the icy fingers squeezing his heart eased their grip when he sensed she was still in the theatre. He teleported to the foyer and found her there.

She turned to face him, her back to the glass doors and the night beyond. The warm lights from the chandeliers did strange things to her hair. Or perhaps not. He frowned. Silver streaks shot through the chestnut, and the more he stared, the more strands turned the colour of stars. Why?

Elissa looked away.

"Where are you going?" he said and took a step towards her, fear turning his blood to icy sludge.

"I'm sorry... I caused so much hurt and I didn't mean to."

"Antoine will be fine and Snow will recover."

She lifted her head and shook it, her silvery eyes filled with sorrow that flowed through the connection between their blood.

"I wasn't talking about them... I was talking about you."

Payne looked at her hair. More of it was silver and he had a horrible feeling he knew why. She was marked now. Tainted.

"I've done terrible things to you too... why didn't you tell me this would happen?" He longed to close the gap between them, run his fingers through her hair and tell her that he would fix it somehow. He would make everything right and he would take care of her if she would only let him. He would be a good mate, and would protect her and Luca.

The boy stirred, opening sleep-filled grey eyes, his expression soft and docile. When he saw Elissa, tears sprang into his eyes and he sobbed. She set him down on his bare feet, crouched and held him, rubbing his back as he cried into her hair, his little fingers buried in it, clinging to her. Payne clenched his fists and then took a step towards them, unable to deny his need to comfort them both.

Elissa looked up at Payne.

Several women appeared on the pavement beyond her, outside the theatre. Payne growled. The little boy tensed in Elissa's arms. She gathered him closer and turned to face the newcomers.

Witches.

A blonde middle-aged woman moved forwards and paused with her foot in the air, close to the boundary of Vampirerotique. She set it down, glared at the stone steps and then up at the facade of the theatre.

"Elissa," she shouted, loud enough for Payne to hear it through the glass.

Elissa took Luca's hand, walked with him to the door and opened it.

Payne's heart broke at the thought she might still leave.

The witches would hurt her if she tried.

"Leave this place of death." The woman stared up at Elissa, flanked by six other witches, all of them dressed in traditional dull black dresses. They were here on business then. "We have come to take you home."

Elissa looked back over her shoulder at him. In the low light, he couldn't see the silver in her hair, and that meant the witches couldn't either. Didn't they know what he had done to her or were they just trying to fool her and lure her out so they could hurt her? Was it as she had said and he had thought, and the spell that cloaked the incubi den had severed her coven's connection to her, so they hadn't felt what he had done to her there and were unaware of it?

Payne stared straight into her eyes, unable to put voice to everything he wanted to tell her. It hurt too much. He could see in her eyes that she longed to go with these witches. She wanted to believe that they would accept her even though he had tainted her, ruined her. She didn't want to be with him, and he couldn't blame her. He could only blame himself.

He had never thought he would find another woman to love, a second chance at having a destined mate. He had never thought he would find a woman that he could love without fear, safe in the knowledge that her feelings and desires were her own, and that she would never turn on him. The phantom's words still haunted him. They had all come true. What had that female seen in his future?

Would Elissa stay with him?

Or would she leave forever?

Elissa looked at her coven.

She took a step back towards Payne. He couldn't believe it, not even when she stopped beside him and slipped her free hand into his, clutching it tightly.

"You would align yourself with wretched bloodsuckers rather than your own kind?" The blonde witch looked as though she wanted to tear Elissa apart for it but she made no move to take the steps and enter the theatre.

They were scared. They knew who lived in this theatre and they feared entering it.

More of Elissa's hair turned silver and Payne knew the witch had noticed it when her eyes narrowed and she spat on the stone steps, muttering something black and foul.

Payne moved in front of Elissa, protecting her as he always would. The witches glared at him and disappeared one by one, but it wasn't over. Elissa's hair had marked her for all to see as tainted and if she ever returned to the fae world, to her home, the witches there would see it and inform her coven. They would wait for her to leave the safety of vampire territory and then they would come after her.

And he would be there to protect her.

Wherever she went, he would be there for her.

He turned to face her. "I'm sorry. I'll talk to Antoine and ask if you can stay here until I find you somewhere you will both be safe."

Elissa frowned. "I have found somewhere like that already."

She had?

Was that why she had been leaving?

She took hold of his hand and smiled into his eyes. "Here, with you. If you'll have us."

Us.

Payne looked down to find a little boy with his head tilted right back, staring up at him. He looked eerily like Payne had as a boy. Did the boy think Payne looked like him too?

"Luca..." Elissa crouched so she was eye level with him. "This is Payne."

Luca stared at him again and then sleepily rubbed his eyes and held his hand out. Elissa gave Payne an expectant look. Payne took the boy's tiny hand in his.

"Nice to meet you." The boy shook his hand and then paused and frowned. He moved underneath Payne's arm and stroked the symbols on his dirty skin, and then looked up at him again. "You're like me. My daddy said I would get these too, when I'm a grown up. Are you my big brother?"

Payne smiled and ruffled his sandy hair. "Something like that, Kid."

It was better he play big brother to the little Hell spawn than treat the small boy as his uncle. It still felt weird to have an uncle who was several hundred years younger than he was.

"Is daddy here too?" Luca looked around him and Elissa caught his shoulders, bringing the boy to face her.

"He had to go away... but Payne is going to take care of us." Elissa smoothed her fingers across the boy's cheek and he smiled at her, dark eyes overflowing with affection. "We're going to live here together... with some other nice people... like a family."

Payne choked.

Elissa frowned up at him and then her expression softened. He cursed the lingering connection between their blood or perhaps it was her natural talents that allowed her to see straight through him to the feelings he was trying to hide. Affection. Fear. Hope. And a lot of confusion and a bit more fear. With another helping of fear on top.

Family?

She stood and Luca settled into her side, resting his head on her leg. She wrapped one arm around him and Payne noticed that she was covering his ear and pressing the other one to her body.

"Just... let him think it for now. Please? He's been through so much," she whispered, her silvery eyes imploring him. "He needs a family."

A family. Payne looked down at Luca. Someone to love him unconditionally. Someone to teach him about the world and being an incubus, and how to control his hungers and embrace his nature. Someone to protect him and keep him safe, and never let anyone hurt him or discover his name and use it against him. Someone who would always be on his side, always there for him, no matter what.

All the things Payne had never had.

Until now.

He looked at Elissa and saw all those things in her as she stared into his eyes, hers full of love and acceptance.

His true mate.

He held his hand out to her and tried to stop it from shaking. "What if it didn't have to be for now... what if it could be forever?"

Elissa's soft lips curved into a beautiful smile and she placed her hand into his. He drew her to him, stepping into her at the same time, caught her cheek with his other hand and tilted her head back so he could see into her eyes. His salvation. His whole world. She had given him everything he had never dared dream of having and he would do the same for her. He would love her forever and raise Luca with her, as a family.

"We'll drive you crazy," she said.

"I know." He smiled.

"You'll never get a moment's peace."

"I know." His smile widened. She would end up giving him peace because he had a suspicion that the females of Vampirerotique would keep her busy for a lot of her time. Kristina was due to birth twins soon and Sera and Chica doted on her. He had noticed the way Sera had looked at Luca tonight. They would be all over him like a rash. He was going to end up spoiled.

"And I'm going to make you submit to me every night."

Payne purred inside at that but put on his best poker face. "You can try, Witch."

She smiled sassily. "And I will succeed, Vampubus."

"Vampubus? Seriously?" He frowned at her.

"Incupire?"

His frown became a black scowl.

"How about... mate?" she said and he was man enough to admit he melted inside a little at the sound of her calling him that, and the thought that she was going to give him the second chance with her that he desired.

He purred aloud now and growled as he gathered her closer. "Mate."

He dipped his head to kiss her.

"Ew." The small voice made him freeze and look down. Luca grinned at him and raised both hands towards him. "Up."

Payne heaved a sigh, already wondering when he would get his witch alone again so he could make up for the last time they had made love and show her that if she stuck with him, he would make it worth her while. He would play her games and give her pleasure she had never known, and he would gladly submit to her, and only her.

He bent, caught Luca under his arms and scooped him up, holding him in the air, causing the young boy to laugh. "Swing me."

Elissa stepped back to give them room and Payne wasn't sure this was a good idea. He didn't know how strong the boy was or whether he would hurt him, but Elissa's soft look of approval said he could do as Luca had asked.

Payne did two full spins with him, sending the boy's legs flying outwards and turning him into a giggling mess. He slowed to a halt, a little dizzy himself, and Elissa came back to them.

Elissa's smile stopped Payne's heart and she stared into his eyes, hers shining with love and happiness. He was new to this parenting thing but he had a feeling that with Elissa tutoring him, he would get the hang of it before long, and Elissa would get her wish, and so would he. They would be family.

Elissa stepped up to him and his heart beat again, thumping hard against his chest with anticipation. She stroked both his and Luca's cheeks, and then looked deep into Payne's eyes, her smile holding and her blood telling him that she would always look at him this way, with unconditional love and devotion.

Payne snaked his free arm around her back and drew her against him, holding both her and Luca close to him.

He would prove to her that he could be a good man, the man she needed him to be, and that she would never have to fear him again if she gave him this chance with her.

He looked down into her eyes and teleported them to his room.

CHAPTER 17

Elissa settled Luca in Payne's four-poster bed, drawing the dark grey covers over him. The room was a little sombre for her tastes, decorated in shades of grey, but it suited Payne for some reason. Luca looked restless and she stroked his brow, sweeping the rogue strands of sandy hair from it and trying to soothe him. He had been through a lot tonight and needed to sleep. They had all been through a lot. She gently used her magic to help him fall asleep again and looked up at Payne as the spell took hold.

Payne stood in the middle of the room, bloodstained and beaten, his eyes locked on her. She blushed under the intensity of his gaze. It wasn't hunger or desire filling them now. There was affection in them as he watched her with Luca, and it warmed her, soothing away her fears. The past few hours had been insane, from Arnaud's attempt to violate her to Payne coming to her rescue, and from landing on the stage in the middle of an extremely naughty act, one she would be asking about later, to being attacked by incubi and threatened by her coven.

Not to mention how rocky things had been between her and Payne. The man fluctuated between cold and warm towards her so rapidly that she couldn't keep track, but she could understand why his mood kept swinging violently from one end of the spectrum to the other. He was afraid.

So was she.

She didn't fear Payne. She already knew in her heart that he would never hurt her or behave as he had the last time they had made love, because she had vowed to never push him over the edge again. She was afraid that she would do or say something to make him feel he would hurt her, or make him feel that they couldn't be together, or she thought he was messed up and a monster. She feared he would leave her now that he had made her fall in love with him.

Now that he had made her want to be his mate with all of her heart.

"So... a dirty theatre... seriously?" She had to say something to break the heavy silence between them and lighten the mood.

He smirked. "I know what you're thinking. I can't accept my incubus nature but I work in a place that deals in erotic shows and sex. I'm only here temporarily to cover for a friend of my family."

That sounded like the Payne she knew. His family had turned their backs on him but he had never been able to turn his on them. He still sought a way to gain their love again. He wanted his family back. A small part of her heart hoped that desire would be fulfilled by having her and Luca in his life. They could be family.

"Not everyone here are vampires... are they?" she said and he shook his head.

She had figured out that there was another fae here, and judging by her appearance and what she had done to the big vampire everyone had called Snow, she was a succubus. It was strange seeing a succubus acting friendly towards an incubus. Elissa had wanted to intervene when the woman had pulled Payne into a hug that had pressed the full length of her rather shapely body against his.

"That's a dark look," Payne said, his smile widening as though he knew what she was thinking. "Chica didn't mean anything by it... but I'm flattered that you're jealous."

Elissa levelled him with a glare. He was reassured more like. She stifled her desire to sigh and stood instead, smoothed her top down and crossed the room to him. She took hold of both of his hands and looked up into his eyes, catching the sparks of blue and gold that shone against the cool grey. How could she make him see that she was here to stay and that she had truly meant what she had told him? There had to be a way to reassure him that she wasn't going to treat him as others had in his life and that her feelings for him would never die, they would only grow over the coming years.

"I meant what I said downstairs, Payne. You don't have to keep doubting me. I want to be your mate."

He closed his eyes and hung his head, a sigh escaping his sensual lips, drawing her gaze to them. "I want that too... but..."

"No buts." Elissa released his left hand and raised hers to his face, cupping his cheek and lifting his chin so he was looking into her eyes again. "I know you... I see you... and I believe you're good mate material and that you'll keep your promise to protect me and Luca... what happened back at the incubi den can't colour our future together. I won't let it. I pushed you too far and I knew the risks. I should have stopped myself. I know how dangerous it was of me to do what I did and I understand you better now. It won't happen again. I trust you, Payne... I want to be with you. I want to be your mate."

"Why?" his voice cracked and her heart went out to him again as his eyes searched hers. He needed more from her and she was willing to give it to him, to take the leap and risk her heart, because he had suffered so much rejection and darkness in his life that he couldn't bring himself to be the one to do it.

Elissa smiled into his eyes. "Because I'm in love with you."

He closed his eyes, snaked his arm around her waist and dragged her against him, clutching her hard against his body. His free hand settled against the back of her head and she shut her eyes as she rested her cheek against his chest, listening to the rapid beat of his heart, feeling him trembling.

"I'm so sorry," he whispered, voice strained and hoarse, laden with emotion. He smoothed his hand through her long hair and she knew he was looking at it, watching as the strands turned silver. Verity had taken to dyeing hers to conceal what she had done.

Elissa would never do that.

"Don't be," she said and drew back enough that she could look up into his eyes. "I don't regret what we did. I want the world to know that I belong to you, and that I'm not ashamed of what we have done... because I love you."

Payne pulled her back to him and kissed her, claiming her lips with such ferocity that she melted into him, lost in how good it felt to be back in his arms and to feel things between them were beginning to find solid even ground again.

She returned his kiss, dancing her lips over his, savouring the way he held her so close to him that she could feel his heart pounding against her breasts. He would never let her go. She knew that and it touched her, soothed her, and she wanted him to know that she felt the same way. She would never let him go. She would always fight for him, even during the times when he hit rock bottom and his past haunted him. She would be there to tell him that she loved him, all of him, and that the past was behind him now, something they would help him deal with together so he could put it to rest and accept that there was good in his life at last.

Elissa paused when she tasted blood and caught hold of his shoulders, pushing him back so she could see his mouth. A single red line cut over his lower lip and the soft flesh around it was swelling. There was a nasty bruise on his left cheek too, and another on the right side of his jaw, that one partially concealed by dried blood.

"You're a mess," she said, frowning as she stepped out of his arms to run an assessing gaze over him. Elissa slipped her hand into his and tugged. "Come on."

He didn't question her as she led him into the dull grey tiled bathroom and released his hand. She closed the door behind him, not wanting Luca to see or hear what was about to happen. She needed to clean Payne up, but more than that, she needed to prove to him that things could be good between them, and that they could make love without worrying he would lose control.

Payne stood immobile in the middle of the cramped bathroom as she unbuttoned his dark bloodstained shirt and pushed it off his shoulders. There were more bruises on his chest and some cuts too. The fight had finished off what she had started on his shirt, completely wrecking it beyond salvation. She dropped the garment to the floor and moved her attention to his jeans. He tensed when she undid his belt and she glanced up into his eyes.

Crimson ringed them but it was the dazzling flecks of gold and cobalt in them that caught her breath. The same colours shimmered over his fae markings, together with dark pink. She had heard what Chica had told him when she had seen those colours on his markings. A mate. Did these colours mean he cared about her and considered her to be his mate already?

Elissa ran her fingers over the line of fae symbols inked along his left shoulder and followed it down over his biceps.

"Pretty colours," she said, afraid of asking him outright whether he returned the feelings she had confessed she felt for him just minutes ago.

"Only one emotion has that shade in it, and it will always be there when I'm with you... even when my incubus nature is in control." He captured her hand and brought it to his lips, pressing a kiss to it.

Elissa raised her eyes to meet his. Her voice shook. "Because you're in love with me?"

"Because I'm in love with you." He nodded and relief swept through her, chasing away the last of her fear. He gathered her into his arms again and kissed her, soft and reverent, filled with the emotion that coloured his markings. Love.

His hands caught the hem of her black halter-top and he pulled it up, severing their kiss for only as long as it took to get the garment off over her head. He dropped it to the floor and pulled her back into his embrace, his mouth capturing hers again, his kiss warming her from head to toe. She skimmed her hands over his upper arms, delighting in the feel of his tensed muscles beneath her fingers, and then ran them down the ridges of his stomach.

Mother earth, she would never get tired of exploring his delicious body.

She undid his belt and then set to work on his buttons, popping each one slowly so her fingers grazed the hard bulge they caged. Payne groaned into her mouth and eased back enough that she could push his dark blue jeans down to his thighs. She broke away and pushed them down to his feet, ending up crouched before him.

Elissa looked up the length of Payne's taut, godly body and moaned, a flood of desire burning up her blood. She bit her lip and then leaned in and licked his cock, running her tongue from root to tip and swirling it around the sensitive crown. He sank his fangs into his lower lip and groaned, the sound strangled and desperate.

His markings remained flushed in blue, gold and pink, swirling and shifting, mesmerising to watch. Did this mean his incubus side was in control now, already at the fore? He wasn't pushing her away though, and she took it as a green light to continue. She wrapped her lips around his cock and took him into her mouth, sucking him as she fondled his heavy sac.

He groaned again and thrust his hips forwards, gently rocking his hard shaft into her mouth, his hands coming down to clutch her shoulder and the back of her head.

"Elissa." He sounded deliciously breathless and lost.

Elissa ran her tongue up the underside of his erection and then rose before him. Blue and gold eyes locked on her, his pupils dark chasms of desire and passion. Mother earth, she wanted him when he looked at her like that, as though he wanted to devour her.

She hastily stripped off her jeans and shoes as he shed the remains of his clothes. Payne advanced on her, forcing her backwards, towards the shower cubicle. It was as small as the one back at Verity's house and it would be cramped, but she was damn well getting him in that shower and wet all over.

Elissa stepped into the cubicle and Payne followed her, his gaze still rooted on her, burning her with its intensity. She fumbled with the controls, nerves and desire combining to make her fingers tremble. Payne calmly reached past her and switched the shower on, his body crowding hers, pressing against it in the most erotic way.

The moment the water was running, he backed her under it and it was a struggle to do what she had come here for. Washing him. She turned around, intent on finding the soap, and he slid his arm around her waist, pulling the full length of her back against his hard front. She moaned and he groaned along with her, the sound bordering on a growl that thrilled her. He grasped her left breast in one hand, palming it and teasing her already hard nipple, and lowered his other to her groin. She gasped as he delved between her plush petals to finger her clitoris, sending hot sparks skittering over her skin. She leaned back against him and rocked her body in time with his fingers, seeking more from him.

Payne ground his cock against her backside, wedging the hot hard length between her buttocks. He dropped kisses on her wet shoulder as he brought her to a shattering climax with his fingers. She breathed hard as he teased her down, gently circling her clitoris now and rolling her nipple between his fingers. He pressed his teeth against her shoulder and she knew what he wanted from her, what he needed. He had lost blood during the fight.

He needed to replenish his strength.

She turned in his embrace, intending to offer her throat to him, and paused when she caught the flicker of fear in his eyes.

Elissa raised both of her hands and settled her palms against his cheeks, holding his face and letting him know that she was there with him and that she wasn't afraid of what might happen because she felt certain that he would retain control this time.

"Make love to me, Payne."

His eyes darted between hers and she did the only thing she could to reassure him that she wanted this and she wasn't afraid. She lured him down to her and kissed him, moulding her mouth over his and capturing the moan that left his lips.

His hands grasped her hips again and he backed her into the corner of the cubicle, out of the spray of the shower. She circled her arms around his neck and pulled herself up his body, settling her legs around his waist. A feral snarl escaped his lips and he kissed her harder, stealing her breath away and reigniting her hunger for him, her need to have his body filling hers and bringing her to climax with him.

He pinned her against the cool tiles and reached between them. She gasped at the feel of the head of his cock rubbing her, teasing her and drawing another flood of arousal from her core. She rocked against him, unable to contain herself, desperate to feel him inside her once more and to make it good this time, to shatter the hold that their last encounter had on Payne.

When he ran his cock downwards this time, Elissa shifted her hips, rocking them forwards so he went further than intended and the head of his shaft slipped into her sheath. She eased down onto him, not giving him a chance to pull out. He groaned against her lips, as still as a statue and taut as a bowstring.

Elissa kissed him, distracting him by running her tongue along the length of his and teasing his fangs, trying to take his focus off the past and bring it to the present. She shifted her feet, drawing him closer to her, deeper into her.

Payne clutched her backside and slowly withdrew, teasing her by almost leaving her before he slid back in, setting a torturous pace that had her writhing in his arms, hungry for more.

He pulled back and stared into her eyes as he moved into her with slow, deliberate strokes, touching every part of her, teasing her towards what she knew would be a mind-blowing orgasm. Elissa held his gaze and ran her fingers through his hair, losing herself in the moment and the beautifully warm look in his eyes. A man had never looked at her like that before, as though she was special and beautiful, as though they were made for each other. She smiled at him, wanting him to see that whatever he was feeling as he moved against her, made love to her, she was feeling it too. From what he had told her about mates, she had been made for him, someone he couldn't control or influence.

Someone he could believe loved him because of who he was not because his incubus side affected her.

She loved him because he was strong, brave, beautiful, and she had never met a man like him.

His fae markings shone brightly and his eyes did too, his incubus side fully in command, but he didn't look as though he was close to losing control. He had never looked more in control. Was it because he knew now that she wouldn't hurt him because she loved him and she had consented to being his mate?

He leaned forwards, slowly driving into her, taking her higher and higher, his hands cool against her hips. She brought her head forwards and pressed her forehead against his, and then kissed him again, sweeping her lips across his and following them with the tip of her tongue. He tilted his head and claimed her mouth, seizing control of the kiss and dominating her as he quickened his pace. He moaned against her lips and she joined him, rocking her hips against his, daring to lose control a little and obey her instincts.

Payne pushed her harder against the tiles and angled his body so he could drive deeper, harder, his pelvis striking her clitoris each time their hips met. She tangled her fingers in his hair and arched her back, tightening around him, seeking more. He grunted and then growled and kissed her desperately. His fangs caught her lower lip and she moaned as he sucked it into his mouth, causing it to tingle and a rush of heat to cascade down her body, settling in her belly. She met each thrust of his cock, using her feet to force him to keep going, to take her harder because she was close now, could almost reach out and grab bliss.

A flash of Payne with his body pounding into hers and his fangs in her throat burst across her mind and she moaned at the image, knowing it was born of her imagination not his. Payne growled and she grabbed his hair, tugged him away from her mouth and forced his head down to her throat. She wanted him to bite her again, ached for the feel of his fangs penetrating her throat and the connection it brought to life between them. It was the push she needed to find release, and she knew he needed it too.

Bewitch

Payne licked her throat and the gentle way he eased his fangs into her flesh surprised her. She had expected him to bite her hard, to strike deep as he had before. The softness of this bite had her soaring higher, light and warm inside, filled with awareness of his feelings and the depth of her own. He loved her.

He pulled on her blood and the rush of it through her veins coupled with the way his long cock eased into her, striking her deep, tipped her over the edge. She cried out his name and clutched him to her throat, the back of her head pressing into the tiles. Fire swept through her, sending her limbs trembling, cascading over her quivering thighs.

Payne buried himself to the hilt inside her and groaned against her throat, pulling on her blood as he spilled himself within her, his hard length throbbing with his release. He wrapped his arms around her, holding her against him, clutching her close as he slowly drank from her, drawing out the hazy warm feeling that flowed through her, adding to her bliss.

She wasn't sure how long they remained there, their bodies intimately entwined, adrift on a warm sea of ecstasy. It was only when Payne released her neck and licked the puncture wounds, his actions gentle, that she came back to the world. He drew back and she smiled into his eyes, not surprised that they were red now, his pupils transformed into their vampire cat-like state.

Elissa ran her thumb across his lower lip, wiping the blood away, and his eyes slowly returned to grey. Not cool grey but warm grey, full of affection and satisfaction. She leaned in and kissed him, keeping things at a slow tempo between them, enjoying the calm and the connection. She could feel him, feel his contentment and happiness via their combined blood, and it felt good.

He had needed to prove to her that they could be together without fear and he had done just that, and she knew things would be good between them again now, and forever. He would never fear that he would lose control and hurt her. He would know now that she was what she had come to realise he longed for her to be—the good that would balance out the bad in his life.

She would always love him and would never hurt him, and she would never let him go. He was her mate.

He withdrew from her, set her down and took hold of her hands. He stepped back, luring her under the warm jet of water. Elissa found the shower gel and set about cleaning him, fussing over his cuts and bruises. He smiled the whole time, his markings never changing from gold, blue and deep pink.

He had fought to protect her. Not just against his grandfather, but against those who had come after them and even against his friends. She had realised the moment they had appeared on the stage of the theatre and he had lost control that he loved her. He had kept his promise to look after her and keep her safe, and he deserved a reward for that.

She looked deep into his eyes, wondering what sort of reward he would like.

He had enjoyed it when kisses had been his reward. Would he still like that now that he had kissed her more times than she could count?

Payne shut the water off and stepped out of the shower. He grabbed a robe and held it out to her. She moved out of the cubicle and took it from him, and paused to watch him as he dried himself off, his body a shifting symphony of masculine power.

Mother earth, she wanted to lick every inch of him.

It was hard to resist the urge, especially when he looked up at her, the gold and blue in his eyes already bright with desire and a lopsided smile telling her he had picked up the wicked images leaping through her head.

Elissa wrapped the robe around her, opened the door and walked out into the main room of Payne's quarters before she pounced on him. She had to check on Luca. She walked to the bed, her gaze settling on Luca where he slept soundly, tucked under the deep silver-grey covers. She would do her best to be a good mother to him, and she felt in her heart that Payne would do all he could to help her and the boy.

Payne's footfalls were quiet on the wooden floor but she could feel his eyes on her, burning her as they always did, igniting a need to turn and step into his arms. He came around her, wearing only a white towel slung low around his hips, and settled his arm across her shoulders, curling his hand around to clutch her upper arm. Elissa leaned into his side, loving the feel of his hard body against hers, warmed all over by thoughts of what lay ahead for them both.

She looked up at Payne and he lowered his eyes to meet hers, stealing her breath with the tender look in them. So much love. How could anyone have ever not loved all of this man? It was both sides of him that made him who he was—protective, loyal, affectionate and beautiful.

A man who deserved everything he desired in life, and she was determined to give him just that.

Payne held Elissa close to him, the deep affection and tenderness in his grey eyes telling her that he would never let either her or Luca go now. He would keep his promise and he would protect them, and love them, forever.

Elissa rewarded him as she always would.

With a kiss.

With her love.

The End

Read on for a preview of the final book in the London Vampires romance series, Unleash!

UNLEASH

～∞～

The vampire raged in his sleep.

His bare torso bowed off the mattress and his powerful muscles strained as he pulled at the heavy cuffs chaining him to the steel posts of the large bed.

When they didn't give, he thrashed his long muscular legs, pulling the black covers down and revealing more of him to her eyes, including the start of a colourful tattoo on his right hip. The lower half of it disappeared beneath his black underwear. She couldn't make out the design from this distance and refused to give in to the temptation to move closer.

She shouldn't be here.

Her master would be angry with her if he discovered she had left her post to be here, unable to keep away.

Snow snarled and twisted his arms in the thick steel and leather restraints, reopening the ragged marks around his wrists and spilling fresh blood. He had been lost to his bloodlust for many weeks now and a few days ago, things had taken a sharp downwards turn, plunging him into the darkest throes of his curse, far worse than any she had witnessed before.

What did he dream to make him turn so violent and wild?

She could see others' dreams but never his.

Her master believed they would prove to be too much for her, and she felt he might have been right to take that ability from her where this vampire was concerned.

She moved a step closer but kept her distance, standing several feet from the end of the bed in his grim black-walled apartment. He had been doing so well recently, gaining ground against his addiction and learning to master it. Now he seemed worse than ever. Lost.

He growled again, the sound pained and feral, like an animal caught in a vicious snare with no hope for escape. His claws scratched at the heavy steel chains of his restraints, blunted by the sheer number of times he had attempted to grasp them.

He thrashed his head and bared his fangs, his face twisting into a dark visage that was so different to his normal appearance. It had startled her the first time he had changed and revealed his darker nature all those countless centuries ago. Part of her had known then that Snow's future would hold more pain than one man could bear, and she had wished she had spared him such a life when she'd had the chance.

Snow twisted and bucked, the ferocity of his thrashing causing the steel posts of his bed to groan against the large bolts that secured them to the floor and ceiling of his room.

She had the oddest urge to go to him and stroke his brow. Why?

Did she hope it would soothe him?

She wanted to soothe him somehow. She knew that. It was why she had come to this dangerous place, cloaked from the eyes of those who resided in the London theatre, Vampirerotique.

She had visited him often over the past few weeks, always remaining in the shadows, shrouded and invisible to those she observed. She had watched the way everyone interacted with Snow, even though he was unconscious most of the time or maddened by rage at the rest.

She knew what this place meant to him and these people, and what he meant to them.

Over the past century, she had witnessed how each event that had occurred at the theatre had changed him. He had been wary at first, watchful, keeping to himself and keeping his distance from all but his brother, but then he had begun to grow closer to the other males who ran Vampirerotique, and then he had taken the first step towards a brighter future without even knowing it.

He had started to consider those at the theatre as his family.

It had surprised her at first and she had been convinced that she was mistaken for many long months, but then she had begun to hope that the new family he had constructed for himself would become his salvation.

She only wished he were lucid enough to hear those who visited him and know their heartfelt wishes, because she was sure he would battle his bloodlust if he knew they all desired him to be well again.

There were new additions to the theatre she felt he would want to meet too.

Babies.

Callum, the black-haired elite male with the striking green eyes, had come to Snow's room one day with a baby cradled in each arm. He had spoken to Snow, who had been unconscious at the time, peaceful, and had shown the babes to him. He had told Snow that he wanted him to get better because he had to meet the twins, and even his wife, the werewolf Kristina, desired it.

It had been difficult to keep her emotions in check that day, watching as Callum talked to Snow, sensing his hope that the male would wake. He had wanted to give Snow a reason to fight and had wanted him to come around in order to ease everyone's minds and lift the burden from their hearts.

She had found a new level of respect for the green-eyed male.

She had also discovered a deep affection for the young female vampire, Lilah. The brunette regularly visited Snow to sit in the wooden chair near the four-poster bed and read to him, keeping vigil at his side whether he was unconscious or raging with bloodlust. Her mate, the sandy-haired elite vampire Javier, often came with her and she knew it was because he feared for his mate and wanted to protect her from Snow if something bad happened.

There were others at the theatre who visited too. A mixed blood male with fair hair and intriguing markings came from time to time, and always apologised. Payne felt responsible for Snow's current state. He wasn't alone in that feeling.

The succubus who was bonded to Javier's younger brother, Andreu, shared Payne's sense of guilt. She had been the one to kiss Snow, stealing his energy and rendering him unconscious.

"Aurora." Snow bucked and growled, his tone dark yet pleading.

She frowned at him. She knew not why he said that word so often but it had drawn her to him that night on the stage of the theatre all those weeks ago, and it drew her again each time he spoke it, as though he was calling out to her. He always spoke that word in a voice edged with pain and she ached to do something to ease his suffering.

She ached to bring him back to the world. He had never suffered like this and she didn't like it. She felt as though he was fading from this world and she could do nothing to stop it from happening. She felt as lost as those who loved him, who spent hours at his side, hoping for him to return to them.

Antoine burst through the mahogany panelled door to her left, his expression revealing his panic as his pale blue eyes sought his older brother. He shoved his long fingers through his wild brown hair and stalked across the room to the bed where it stood against one of the shorter sides of the apartment, opposite the bathroom at her back.

"Snow?" he whispered, fear mixed with hope in his voice.

Snow failed to respond. He lay still on the bed, but not unconscious.

Antoine neatened the black bedclothes, covering his brother's legs and drawing them over his waist to hide his black boxer shorts and give him some shred of dignity. He heaved a sigh and went to the ebony nightstand beside the bed, retrieving the wad of cotton wool and tearing a piece from it.

He wetted it with something from a glass bottle and then rounded the bed to Snow's feet. She watched on as he cleaned the dried blood from Snow's ankles and feet, his actions careful and speaking of the deep affection that he held for his brother.

She felt sorry for him. Sympathy. An emotion well within her grasp. She had felt it for Snow too once and it had changed the course of her life, and she was no longer sure it had been for the better. Perhaps she had thought it a long time ago.

Antoine finished cleaning Snow's ankles and wearily tossed the soiled cotton wool into the overflowing waste bin near the black nightstand. She hated the colour of Snow's room. Everything in it was morbid, funerary, and left her feeling it was a tomb for the living dead.

A grave for a man who was waiting to die.

Antoine tunnelled his fingers through his hair again, shoving it out of his face, and sat on the edge of the mattress on Snow's right. Only he was brave enough to sit so close to him, and she admired him for it and the faith he had in his brother, especially after everything that had happened between them.

Snow's younger brother sighed again, the sound as weary as his appearance made him look. He was normally a neat and elegant man, dressing in fine tailored shirts, polished Italian leather shoes, and perfectly pressed slacks. Now he wore crumpled black trousers and had fastened only the middle three buttons of his charcoal shirt, the tails of it left to hang outside his trousers. His feet were bare.

"Snow?" Antoine leaned forwards, planted his right hand against the mattress and stroked his brother's brow with his left hand, clearing the ribbons of white hair from it.

Again the urge came, the strange need to mimic that action he did so often when he visited his brother.

Another urge joined it as she sensed Antoine's pain and knew his secret fear. He feared that Snow wasn't strong enough to pull through this time. His brother had been seeking his death for centuries and Antoine was afraid that Snow would take this as his chance to escape the pain of his life and find eternal peace.

The sympathy she felt for Antoine grew stronger, consuming her, and she wanted to reveal herself to him and ease his suffering by reassuring him that his brother would not leave him and he would wake soon.

She would see to it.

The door opened again and Sera entered, blinking sleep from her forest green eyes and struggling to tie her long blonde hair into a knot at the back of her head. She rubbed her eyes and then fastened her dark red silk robe around her waist, covering her black slip.

"Antoine," she said softly and her mate turned and looked over his shoulder at her, his pale blue eyes flooded with fatigue and pain. She opened her arms to him, crossed the room and wrapped them around his shoulders. He settled his head against her chest and she ran her fingers through his hair. "You need to rest."

"I cannot... not while..." He turned and buried his face against her, and she tightened her grip on him, holding him close and dipping her head to press a kiss to his hair.

"He will be well," she whispered and continued to stroke the shorter hair at the back of his head. "Give him time. You need to rest too... this has all been too much for you and I don't want—"

Sera cut herself off.

She knew what the female vampire wanted to say but couldn't. She feared that Antoine would follow his brother and lose himself to the bloodlust he fought to keep at bay if he didn't keep his strength up, both physically and spiritually.

Sera stepped back and took hold of Antoine's hands. He looked up at her and nodded, and she released him. He rose to his feet and then pressed one knee into the mattress and leaned over Snow. He pressed a kiss to his brother's forehead.

"Don't you dare give up." His voice cracked and tears filled his eyes.

Antoine straightened, turned, and walked swiftly out of the room. Sera stroked Snow's cheek and sighed.

"You'd better be listening to him, big guy. You know he can't live without you. None of us can." She brushed her knuckles along his straight jaw and then turned and followed her mate from the room, closing the door behind her.

Another door closed and she was alone with Snow again. His breathing quickened and she knew what was coming. He had been still for long enough, had regained some of his strength, and was now going to use it in an attempt to break free of his bonds.

It was always the same.

He would go in circles, a pattern she had learned by heart over the past few weeks. He would fight, and then rest, and then fight again, and then take a shorter rest as his frustration mounted, and then he would fight harder than ever, and fail to free himself.

The end result was always the same too. Exhaustion, leading to unconsciousness. Sometimes he was out for days. Other times it was only minutes before he began the cycle again.

Snow turned savage, the change between placid and violent swift and startling. The chains rattled and then groaned under the pressure of his harsh movements on the bed. He tugged at them, powerful body bowing off the mattress and his muscles bunching and tightening as he fought the restraints that kept him flat on his back. Helpless.

The cuffs bit into his ankles and wrists, and his flesh seeped droplets of blood that the thick restraints then smeared across his skin, renewing the stains. He snarled and fought, lashing out with his fists and feet, shaking the whole bed. The metal sliced deeper into his wrists, until rivulets spilled down his bloodied arms and soaked into the black sheets. Crimson tainted the overlong strands of his white hair and stained his shoulders and neck

Unleash

too. His eyes rolled open and then back again, a flash of scarlet irises and thin black vertical slits for pupils.

They had been red since the night he had first stirred after the incident on the stage, a sign that his bloodlust still had a strong hold over him.

They were red even when he was unconscious.

His lips parted, revealing enormous fangs.

She pitied him even as she despised him.

Her feelings had never been as muddled as they were now.

He sniffed and suddenly stilled, and a prickle of awareness ran down her spine. He had sensed her. How?

He bellowed in fury and thrashed violently against his restraints, causing the metal post that secured his left ankle to bend slightly. Fresh blood ran over his ankles, coating the steel cuffs. He fought harder and it pained her because she knew that after this time he would fall unconscious.

She should leave.

Her place wasn't here.

She knew that in her heart, but that same heart had urged her to come to him when she had felt his pain and his distress. Now that she had seen how fiercely the bloodlust gripped him, she couldn't turn her back on him. She needed to do something to help him.

She could calm him, but if anyone discovered what she had done, she would have damned herself.

She edged closer to him, her heart thumping crazily in her breast, her gaze locked on him and watching for an attack even though she knew he couldn't break his bonds and reach her. He tried to lunge for her, his blunt claws scratching at the air. His red eyes shot to her, focused and sharp, locked on her like lasers.

Her stomach fluttered but her step didn't falter.

She swallowed her trembling heart and reached out to him, afraid that he would somehow manage to injure her but strengthened by the knowledge that she might be able to do something to crack the hold his bloodlust had on him and guide him back to his loved ones.

She stopped at his side and dared to lift her cloak so he could see her, hoping it would calm him and he would see she wasn't a threat to him. She gently lowered her hand, intending to touch his face as the female, Sera, and his brother had.

Snow snapped at her fingers and tried to bite her, his sharp fangs gleaming in the low light from the lamps around the black room.

She changed course and settled her hand on his bare chest instead. His powerful heart thundered hard against her palm. A heavy tribal beat.

It accelerated as she stood over him and then she shifted her eyes to meet his and it began to slow to a more gentle sedate rhythm.

He blinked slowly, long dark lashes shuttering his crimson eyes before lifting again to reveal them to her.

She whispered to him, soft words in a tongue that was probably foreign to him now.

A song to soothe him.

She sung of soaring in a midnight sky, dancing over mountains, and reaching towards the horizon, beyond the snowy valley and the frozen waterfall.

Snow stilled, his expression turning docile, and she bravely moved her hand to his face, stroking his stubbly cheek as she softly sung to him of a prince and his love, his kingdom on earth while hers was in heaven.

Two worlds too far apart.

Two hearts too close to part.

Snow blinked languidly again and then his eyelids drooped and he settled heavily into the bed, his arms lax and hands hanging limply from the cuffs. She focused on his wrists, on the red lines that slashed across them, and willed them to heal.

She brushed her fingertips across his cheek and whispered, "Sleep... dream... remember who you were."

Voices sounded in the hall and she tore herself away from him, stroking his cool cheek one last time and leaving a streak of beautiful colours on his skin.

She stepped back and spread her wings, her eyes still locked on him.

The vampire slumbered peacefully, and it warmed her heart and gave her hope.

"Take more care of yourself. I will be watching."

The door behind her opened, throwing golden light across her and Snow, though she cast no shadow upon him.

She was already gone from this world.

She stood at the edge of a white battlement, staring down at the world far below her, distant and indistinct.

It was done.

Now she had to leave him alone or her master would discover that she had sinned again because of Snow.

He would never forgive her this time.

UNLEASH

A powerful vampire lost deep in his bloodlust, Snow is a savage animal, mindless with rage and a thirst for violence, and trapped with no hope of awakening from an endless nightmare… until a song draws him up from the abyss, restoring his sanity but leaving him haunted by the sweet feminine scent of lilies and snow, and fragmented familiar lyrics.

When the mysterious and beautiful songstress reappears in Snow's room at Vampirerotique, she awakens a fierce protective streak and stirs dark desires that drive him to claim her as his female, even when he knows his touch will destroy her innocence.

A single forbidden taste is all it takes to unleash emotions in Aurora that she shouldn't possess, tearing her between duty and desire, and luring her into surrendering to her wildfire passion and embracing hungers that burn so hotly they threaten to consume them both.

One act of kindness can lead to one thousand acts of sin though, each a black mark against the bearer's soul and another grain of sand that slips through an hourglass. The clock is ticking and time is almost up. Can beauty save the beast?

Available now in ebook and paperback

ABOUT THE AUTHOR

Felicity Heaton is a New York Times and USA Today best-selling author who writes passionate paranormal romance books. In her books she creates detailed worlds, twisting plots, mind-blowing action, intense emotion and heart-stopping romances with leading men that vary from dark deadly vampires to sexy shape-shifters and wicked werewolves, to sinful angels and hot demons!

If you're a fan of paranormal romance authors Lara Adrian, J R Ward, Sherrilyn Kenyon, Kresley Cole, Gena Showalter, Larissa Ione and Christine Feehan then you will enjoy her books too.

If you love your angels a little dark and wicked, her best-selling Her Angel romance series is for you. If you like strong, powerful, and dark vampires then try the Vampires Realm romance series or any of her stand alone vampire romance books. If you're looking for vampire romances that are sinful, passionate and erotic then try her London Vampires romance series. Or if you like hot-blooded alpha heroes who will let nothing stand in the way of them claiming their destined woman then try her Eternal Mates series. It's packed with sexy heroes in a world populated by elves, vampires, fae, demons, shifters, and more. If sexy Greek gods with incredible powers battling to save our world and their home in the Underworld are more your thing, then be sure to step into the world of Guardians of Hades.

If you have enjoyed this story, please take a moment to contact the author at **author@felicityheaton.com** or to post a review of the book online

Connect with Felicity:
Website – http://www.felicityheaton.com
Blog – http://www.felicityheaton.com/blog/
Twitter – http://twitter.com/felicityheaton
Facebook – http://www.facebook.com/felicityheaton
Goodreads – http://www.goodreads.com/felicityheaton
Mailing List – http://www.felicityheaton.com/newsletter.php

FIND OUT MORE ABOUT HER BOOKS AT:
http://www.felicityheaton.com

Printed in Great Britain
by Amazon